The Penderghast Puzzle Protectors

(A Brilliant, Minnesota Mystery)

by

Julie Seedorf

Copyright © 2016 by Julie Seedorf

For information, email **Cozy Cat Press**, cozycatpress@aol.com or visit our website at: www.cozycatpress.com

COZY CAT
PRESS

ISBN: 978-1-939816-80-1
Printed in the United States of America

Cover design by Paula Ellenberger
http://www.paulaellenberger.com/

10 9 8 7 6 5 4 3 2 1

I dedicate this book to my husband, who puts up with my quirky and weird personality. Thank you for loving me.

ACKNOWLEDGEMENTS

Thank you to Annie Sarac and *The Editing Pen* for making me look good with their editing skills, knowing I am always comma challenged. Thank you to Patricia Rockwell and Cozy Cat Press for believing in me and my writing. Thank you to my "soon to be" new grandson Dylan for supporting my writing and also being an avid reader, helping me with my ideas.

To my amazing readers who support my creative imagination by reading my books and to my friend Donna who has always accepted my quirkiness and encourages me and accepts the creative part of me always. Also I would like to thank The Interchange in Albert Lea, Minnesota, one of my favorite hang outs, for letting me use their name in my book. The Interchange's coffee, wine and food and customer service always put a huge smile on my face.

CHAPTER ONE

Jezabelle Jingle peeked out the front window of her Victorian home. She looked for Mr. Warbler but hadn't seen him since yesterday.

Jezabelle kept an eye on the neighborhood. She knew the exact time Phoebe Harkins took out the trash. Every morning at exactly 9:00 a.m., Phoebe's front door would open, Jasper the dog would bound out the door, do the downward dog stretch on the porch, and run to Mr. Warbler's yard to relieve himself. Phoebe would walk out the door, holler at Jasper, and continue to the curb with the trash.

Every evening at exactly 10:00 p.m., Rock Stone (Jezabelle didn't understand why anyone with a last name like Stone would name their son Rock) would drive into his driveway with his old truck, rev the engine twice, and have a last puff on his cigarette before he went inside for the night.

Miranda Covington was another matter altogether. She never did anything on time. Occasionally, Jezabelle would see her running out of her house at 2:00 a.m. Miranda would turn left and dash down the sidewalk to the west. Jezabelle never could see where she was going. It was too dark. Miranda would return minutes later only to leave again in an hour or two. Miranda never left her house at the same time, she was never gone the same amount of time, and she never left her house during the day.

Jezabelle wasn't nosy; she took care of her neighborhood. She was concerned. Today, Mr. Warbler was off-schedule. Every day at exactly 6:00 a.m., 1:00 p.m., 4:00 p.m. and, depending on whether it was dark or not as it always stayed light longer in the summer, 8:00 p.m., Mr. Warbler could be seen in his yard checking on his bird feeders and feeding the squirrels. In fact, right now the squirrels were scurrying in and out of the bushes waiting for Mr. Warbler's arrival, but Mr. Warbler had not fed his squirrels today.

Never one to leave a stone unturned, Jezabelle donned her hat and her sweater and headed to Mr. Warbler's house. She stepped over the puddle left after the rain the night before, and avoided a car cruising too fast, spattering water in her direction as the car hit the puddles in the street. Jezabelle moved swiftly and with purpose.

Jezabelle knocked and listened. *Was that someone screaming for help?*

"Help! Someone help me!"

It was Mr. Warbler. Something was wrong. She tried the doorknob, but it was locked. "I'm coming! I'm coming!" Jezabelle ran to the back door. It too was locked. Jezabelle might be old, but she knew she was wiry. With eyes on the side window, Jezabelle ran, jumped high, grabbed the windowsill, hung on, and tried to open the window. The window was locked.

"Help! Please don't leave. Help me!"

Jezabelle heard Mr. Warbler screaming. He didn't sound as if he was hurt, but he sounded as if he was in trouble. She had to do something. She could get her baseball bat and break a window. She immediately nixed that idea. It might be too messy. She might cut herself climbing through the window and she didn't like blood, especially her own.

She could call the fire department, but maybe Mr. Warbler had just locked himself in a closet and couldn't get out. He would feel foolish. She wouldn't call the fire department. Then she remembered Max. Max was Mr. Warbler's faithful hound. Max had a mind of his own and Mr. Warbler had tired of his willfulness. Max always wanted to visit the outdoors at inopportune times, so Mr. Warbler had put in a doggy door. No one kept track of Max. Max had a girlfriend on the other side of town and he often left for days at a time to visit her. Max found his way home whenever he felt like it. Mr. Warbler always left the doggie door unhinged. Since Jezabelle was a petite old woman, she thought she would try Max's doggie door.

Jezabelle got down on her knees, checked to make sure no one was watching, and then crawled into Mr. Warbler's house. She could hear him hollering, so she followed the sound. What she saw made her stop and break out in an uproarious laugh. There in the parlor was Mr. Warbler, hanging down from the ceiling, his body stuck between floors with just his feet dangling and the upper half of his body invisible, stuck in the upstairs bedroom.

"Don't you laugh, Jezabelle. Just get me out of here!" bellowed Mr. Warbler.

Jezabelle had to compose herself before she could speak. She laughed so hard the tears ran down her cheeks. "And how am I supposed to do that? Do you have a ladder?"

"A ladder is not going to help. I'm stuck so tight my belly is rolled over on the floor up here. You need to get help."

Well, thought Jezabelle, *if that was what he wanted she would call the fire department*. It wasn't her fault if Mr. Warbler looked like a fool. Jezabelle broke out in laughter again and quickly snapped a picture of Mr. Warbler's lower torso with her cell phone. These newfangled phones were good for something. It would make a nice picture for the front page of the *Brilliant Times Chronicle*. So first, Jezabelle flashed, and then she dialed 9-1-1.

CHAPTER TWO

Jezabelle heard the sirens and the roar of the fire trucks as they turned the corner at Roosevelt and Strong. Shaking her head, she concluded the neighborhood hadn't had so much excitement since Roland Door got his head stuck in a bucket while he was washing his windows. Roland fell, the ladder fell, the bucket fell, and Roland's head was stuck.

Jezabelle heard Mr. Warbler muttering. "Was that a curse word I heard up there, Mr. Warbler?" asked Jezabelle. Jezabelle again smiled, then laughed so loud that the firefighters now coming in the door thought she was the one needing help. She had to point to the ceiling to draw their attention to Mr. Warbler, at which point the firefighters too began laughing uproariously having a hard time holding on to their equipment.

After the mirth passed, the firefighters rushed up the stairs to see what they had to do to free Mr. Warbler. Jezabelle followed. First they tried grease. It didn't help. They could not shrink his belly. Evidently, he had just come out of the shower, put on his pants, and was walking across the room to get his shirt when the floor gave way.

Red Hannahan shook his head. Turning to Jet Pillager, he barked an order. "Get the chainsaw!"

"Chainsaw!" Mr. Warbler's quivering voice spouted out the words.

"Don't worry, Warbler," Red answered, "we just have to cut a bigger square out of the floor and take you out with it."

Jezabelle said to Mr. Warbler, "Pretend you're one of your birds and sing loud—you won't even notice the chainsaw." She held up her phone camera and instructed the men, "Say cheese!" Jezabelle clicked a couple of times, making sure she captured the scared look on Mr. Warbler's face, and the smile Red Hannahan was trying to keep off *his* face because of the situation, before turning and going back downstairs to join the other firefighters. She knew this would be a perfect front-page picture for the *Brilliant Times Chronicle*. The town of Brilliant was always glad when the news of the day was on the front page in pictures. They wouldn't have to take the time to read the article on this one. The picture said it all.

Jet handed the chainsaw to Red. George Grifter and Cal Phillips, the other firefighters who'd stayed downstairs waiting for instructions, set up a ladder under Mr. Warbler.

George Grifter gave directions to Mr. Warbler. "Now, Warbler, when they cut you out, I'll guide your feet to the top of the ladder. Hold steady to what's left of the floor and then we'll lift you down. Got that?"

"What...? Are you sure? Be careful." Mr. Warbler's body shook, just like his voice.

"We got this, Warbler," Red answered as he started the chainsaw.

Jezabelle heard the saw cutting through the floor. At the last minute, Jet covered Mr. Warbler's head with a cloth so no flying wood chips would hit his skin.

She heard Mr. Warbler muttering under the cloth, "It's almost over; it's almost over."

The final cut could be heard. Cal Phillips grabbed Mr. Warbler's legs and steadied them on the ladder as the final cut was made. Mr. Warbler, feeling as if his body were encased in a picture frame, panicked and began flailing his arms. The surprise move knocked Cal Phillips off the ladder onto George Grifter. Both men tumbled to the floor with the ladder on top of them. Mr. Warbler's chubby wood-encased body, not having the ladder underneath his feet any more, fell straight down to the first floor and tumbled on top of Jezabelle.

Max the dog chose that moment to run into the house through his dog door. Seeing all the people on the floor, he ran over, barking excitedly, and jumped on top of Mr. Warbler and Jezabelle. The firefighters picked themselves up off the floor and quickly ran to help the two up. All they could see of Jezabelle's tiny body was her feet sticking out from under Mr. Warbler's wood-encased body.

Jet and Red ran down the stairs the minute Mr. Warbler slipped out of the grasp of Cal. "Both of you grab Warbler and lift him off Jezabelle!" Jet instructed.

"I can get up myself; I don't need any help," Mr. Warbler advised, trying to sit up. The wood around his body tilted him right back down on top of Jezabelle. Still, there was no sign of life from Jezabelle.

"This is no time to argue!" Red yelled, grabbing one arm and nodding at Jet to grab Mr. Warbler's other arm. Mr. Warbler, being a man of large weight, almost slipped out of their grasp. Cal and George got behind Mr. Warbler's body and pushed him upward until between the four of them they had him standing.

Max licked Jezabelle's face.

Eyes still closed, Jezabelle pushed Max's nose away from her face. "Robert, I told you, no more kisses tonight. You smell like beef sticks."

Jet kneeled down and tapped Jezabelle's face. "Jezabelle, we're calling an ambulance."

At the word *ambulance*, Jezabelle's eyes popped open. "Ambulance? Did something happen to Robert?" She looked around the room with confusion in her eyes.

"No, no Robert," Mr. Warbler answered.

"Why Warbler, why are you wearing a picture frame?" Jezabelle's face broke out in a smile.

"You don't remember?" Jet asked her, helping her sit up.

Jezabelle looked around the room and then up at the ceiling. "Oh, that's right. I had to save Warbler. He was hanging around." She looked at him in concern. "Warbler, I didn't realize you were having problems. That's a strange way to try to kill yourself."

Mr. Warbler, having sat down a little way from Jezabelle, tried to stand up but the wood surrounding him hit the edge of the wall and knocked him back down. "Kill myself? My floor must have been weak."

"That's absurd. I think you've been feeding too many birds and you've gone nutty." Jezabelle held out her hand to Red to help her stand.

"Let's get you two to the hospital to get checked out. We called the Brilliant Ambulance once we saw what was happening and they just arrived," Cal announced.

"But, but…," Mr. Warbler protested.

"I've called Chief Hardy and he'll want to see what we have here. It doesn't look like your floor was weak, it looks like someone cut a hole out of your floor and put a throw rug over it," Jet said, leading Jezabelle out the door. "You can tell us all about this Robert that you thought was kissing you, Jezabelle."

"You've never heard of Robert Redford?" Jezabelle muttered, letting them lead her to the ambulance.

CHAPTER THREE

"You appear to be fine, Jezabelle." Dr. Winkler wrote in his chart while addressing his patient who was sporting a tiny bruise on her leg from the floor that had framed Mr. Warbler and that had then hit her when he came tumbling down on top of her.

"Of course, I'm fine—takes a little more than a Warbler to take me down," Jezabelle answered, dusting off her clothes. "Looks like a little of the ceiling plaster seems to have given me a bath too."

"The plaster was knocked on the floor from the ceiling when Warbler's legs came through," Red Hannahan informed her as he came into the room followed by Chief of Police, Hank Hardy.

"Doc says you're okay, Jezzy." Hank Hardy was the only person in Brilliant who got away with calling Jezabelle "Jezzy." They had been sweet on one another in high school and to Hank Hardy she would always be his Jezzy no matter how old they were. The courtship hadn't worked out, but the fondness they felt for one another had lasted through the years.

"What are you doing here, HH?" Jezabelle used her nickname for the Police Chief. "Didn't know you covered floor failures too. I kept telling Warbler he needed to lose some weight—too many of those banana splits from the *Creamy Cow*, but he didn't listen. I warned him these old houses have weak floors in places."

Hank Hardy and Red Hannahan shared a concerned look between them before Hank answered Jezabelle. "It was no accident, Jezzy. It looks like someone cut a large square out of the floor. The strange thing was that they must have known how the house was built."

"That's impossible," replied Jezabelle. "That house, like mine and all the others on the street, are over one hundred years old. And they've always been in good shape. The owners have kept them up. Are you telling me we have a one-hundred-year-old cutting up floors?"

"Here's the thing," Red Hannahan interrupted. "That exact square of floor was framed in a square, not like the normal joists in a house. That frame was made for exactly that piece of floor."

Hardy nodded his head in agreement. "The perpetrator pulled up that particular floor board without disturbing the ceiling below. That's why Warbler didn't notice it from the living room underneath the bedroom."

"And when they did, they pulled the area rug over to hide the hole. Mr. Warbler stepped on the rug and went right through the floor. The square was just big enough for part of his rotund body to go through but the solid framing of the floor and his stomach wouldn't give way for the rest." Red Hannahan smiled, remembering the picture of Mr. Warbler hanging through the ceiling.

Jezabelle wrinkled her nose, puzzled by the events of the day. " Do you suppose the entire floor is framed like that? And why would someone want a piece of Mr. Warbler's floor?"

Hank Hardy ignored the question and answered with one of his own, "Did you see anything suspicious or anyone you didn't recognize around Mr. Warbler's house today?"

"Other than Miranda Covington actually putting her garbage out at the correct time so she didn't have to run down the street after the garbage truck in her high heels and scanty nighties? Nope, can't say I did." Jezabelle smiled sweetly at the men, remembering that Mr. Warbler was the only one she saw doing something suspicious the day before. Jezabelle decided to keep that little bit of news to herself so she could investigate before she told the police. After all, she didn't want to put Mr. Warbler in a bad light, them being neighbors and all. "Nope, nothing."

"Do you want us to call your niece over in Fuchsia to stay with you tonight to make sure you don't have any after-effects from Mr. Warbler landing on you?" Hank asked Jezabelle.

"I'm fine; Delight has all she can do right now keeping Ella out of trouble. Seems she's in love with some mysterious guy, and Delight has yet to figure out with whom," Jezabelle added, "How's Warbler?"

Both men chuckled. "He's mad as a wet hen that someone stole his floor and somehow the picture already came out on the website of the *Brilliant Times Chronicles*. Apparently it's going to be on the front page of the paper tomorrow morning. He seems to think you sent the picture," Red concluded.

Jezabelle feigned surprise, remembering the snap and the zip as the picture left her phone to the *Chronicle's* address right before Warbler landed on top of her. "Me? Must have been one of those paparazzi types we have in Brilliant. Warbler just doesn't want anyone to know he was crushing on me. Get me out of here. After the day I've had, I think I need the Brilliant Bistro. I'll even buy."

CHAPTER FOUR

The Brilliant Bistro was hopping when Jezabelle, Hank, and Red entered the coffee/wine house. Jiffy Jacks hurried over to the trio. Jiffy owned the Brilliant Bistro. His real name was John Jacks but he got the nickname Jiffy because when he first opened the Bistro he would always greet the customers with the phrase, "I'll be with you in a jiffy." People heard it so often it earned him the name of Jiffy.

"I heard the sirens. Whose house burned down this time?" Jiffy whispered.

Jezabelle put her hand on Jiffy's arm. "Relax, Jiff, you can read all about it on the *Brilliant Times Chronicle* website and on the front page of the paper in the morning."

Red laughed. "Yup, no fire just some bird hanging out and we had to rescue him."

The trio broke into loud laughter making the other patrons in the coffeehouse look up from their coffee and sweets. During the day, the Bistro was a coffeehouse, and in the evening it turned into a wine bar with entertainment. Jiffy Jacks got the idea when he traveled around Minnesota and visited the Interchange in Albert Lea, Minnesota. He thought it was a brilliant idea, so he expanded his coffeehouse adding a wine bar to mimic the Interchange.

The Bistro was a classic older building renovated to its original detail when the town was built. It had been the original drugstore in the community and it housed an old soda fountain. Jiffy Jacks made use of the soda fountain and added an original antique wooden bar from the old saloon in the city. The old saloon had been renovated into a senior citizens' center. How the bar had gotten from the old saloon to the basement of the Bistro baffled Jiffy Jacks. But Jiffy took advantage of it and used it for his wine bar. Behind the bar was the original bar mirror that was said to have hung behind the old saloon in Brilliant and had been found in the old livery stable that was now a restaurant. The old buildings made people feel they had stepped back in time to the late 1800s, early 1900s.

Brilliant, at that time, was said to have housed some of the smartest minds in Minnesota, thus the brilliant minds decided to name the town after themselves.

Jezabelle moved to have a seat at the only open table in the Bistro. "I'll have an espresso. That should set me on my toes."

Red laughed and teasingly explained to Jiffy, "She got a little smashed this morning."

"Smashed? Jezabelle you always hold it to one glass of wine," Jiffy exclaimed, shocked at what he had heard.

Jezabelle was about to protest when she saw the twinkle in Red's and Hank's eyes. "Yup, smashed and framed so they hauled me off to the man in the little white coat," she said, playing along with the joke.

A look of horror popped up on Jiffy Jacks' face. "You didn't? You tried to put her away?"

Hank patted Jiffy on the back. "Relax, Jiff, she had a little accident, and we had Dr. Winkler check her out. A little problem with a falling floor but, as you can see, our Jezzy here is as good as old." Hank couldn't resist taking a little jab at Jezabelle's age. It was a standing joke between the two old friends. Their birthdays were on the same day, and Jezabelle was two hours older than Hank.

Jezabelle opened her mouth to protest Hank's words when his police radio crackled. Hank walked to the edge of the room to listen and not disturb the rest of the customers who all had their ears open, trying to listen to Hank's conversation. Small towns were one big family, and everyone was interested in what everyone else was doing.

"Jezzy, I'll give you a ride home. It seems my team found something at the house that's for sale down the block from you."

Jezabelle stood up. "Guess my espresso will have to wait. Did that darn cat get in that house again? I call it Shifty. I saw it wiggle in through the porch window of that house one day. Apparently the window was open a little. I called the realtor and he couldn't find the cat inside the house, but he made sure the porch window was tight."

"I think they found more than a shifty cat, Jezzy." Hank took her arm to escort her out of the Brilliant Bistro while turning to Red. "See ya later, Red. We might have to interview all of you guys who freed Warbler. Warbler's fall might have been attempted murder."

CHAPTER FIVE

When Hank Hardy pulled into the driveway of 6200 Roosevelt Street, Steve Straight, Hanna Hardy, Jeb Jardene, and Snoop Steckle were waiting for them.

Steve, better known as Stick because he was tall and thin as a stick, Hanna Hardy, Hank Hardy's daughter, and Jeb Jardene, made up the rest of the police force of Brilliant, Minnesota. Snoop Steckle was editor and reporter for the *Brilliant Times Chronicle*.

"What do we have here?" Hank asked his crew.

Stick glanced at Jezabelle. "Jezabelle, nice to see you're okay but I'd suggest you head on home."

"It's my neighborhood and I almost got framed earlier. I think I'll stay." Jezabelle planted her feet firmly on the ground to let them know she was staying.

"It's okay, Stick," Hank said. "Maybe Jezabelle can identify the dead body since none of you know who it is and he didn't have any identification on him."

Jezabelle's eyes opened wide at the mention of a dead body. "You found a dead body in that empty house? No one's lived there for ages, not since Annabelle passed away. Her daughters cleared it out and it's been up for sale."

"You've never seen anyone over here?" Hanna Hardy asked.

"Well, just Max and Jasper. The two dogs would rendezvous in the backyard and hide in the bushes from Warbler and Phoebe." With a twinkle in her eye, Jezabelle suggested, "I think Jasper is really a Jasperine since he had puppies a few months back. Shocked Phoebe. She found homes for the puppies but never figured out that Max was the father. I knew what they were doing in those bushes." Jezabelle chuckled.

Snoop Steckle broke into the conversation, ready to record what they were saying. "Can you tell me was it murder or an accident? What's the dead body telling you?"

Jeb Jardene answered, "The body is telling us it's dead. Anything more you want to ask that we won't answer?"

Hank Hardy turned to Snoop while trying to keep a straight face. "I'll give you the scoop tomorrow when we've had a chance to investigate. For now, this is a crime scene and it's time for you to leave. Hanna, escort Snoop to his car."

As Snoop was getting in his car, Jezabelle gave a yell, "And don't forget to put that great picture of Mr. Warbler on the front page of the paper. He'll be disappointed if you don't."

Turning back to Hank, Jezabelle asked, "Don't you think it's strange that with all this hoopla none of my other neighbors have come out of their houses to see what's going on?"

"Warbler's resting after his ordeal. And the rest of your neighbors aren't home," Hanna answered.

"Are you sure? Phoebe's always home and nosy, and Miranda never leaves her house during the day."

Hank took Jezabelle's arm and led her toward the house. "We've got it covered; nothing for you to worry about. Let's see if you know who this is lying on the basement floor."

"Basement floor—how did they get in the basement?" Jezabelle pointed to the outside covered basement door. "It's been sealed up for years. That daughter of Annabelle's sealed it up because Annabelle was always trying to go down in the basement to find the food she thought she'd canned years ago. She lived in the past, way back in the past."

Jezzy stopped short when they entered the house through the front door. A big gaping hole stood in the middle of the hardwood floor in the living room of the old house. Jezabelle halted and cautiously moved to the hole, peering down into the basement. Hank caught up to Jezzy and grabbed her arm to make sure she didn't lose her balance and end up alongside the victim on the cold basement floor.

A ladder had been lowered down into the opening in the hardwood floor. Jezabelle looked down into the hole before turning to the others. "Did the floor rot out? I thought this house was in great shape last time I was here visiting Annabelle."

"Do you recognize him, Jezabelle?" Jeb asked.

Jezabelle shook her head. "Can't say that I do. Good looking guy though, if he didn't have that gash in his head." She looked carefully through the hole in the floor again. The body was lying on its back in a twisted position, having been left the same way it was when the victim fell through the floor.

"I'll have Hanna escort you home and check your house." Hank turned and instructed Hanna, "Take Jezabelle home and make sure her floors are still there. Apparently we have a floornapper and, until we surmise otherwise, a possible murderer running around."

Jezabelle wrinkled her nose and peered at Hank through squinty eyes. "Floornapper?"

"This piece of flooring was cut out the same as Mr. Warbler's. That's all you need to know for now." Hank gestured for Hanna to lead Jezabelle out of the house.

CHAPTER SIX

Jezabelle lifted up the curtain just enough so no one could see her peeking out. Checking to make sure the police crew were busy with the hearse that had pulled up to Annabelle's house, she picked up a piece of apple pie she'd made earlier in the day and stepped out of the house. She was crossing the street to Mr. Warbler's house when she heard a loud "Woo hoo!" hailing her down. Phoebe Harkins was standing on her step trying to get Jezabelle's attention.

Hearing the words "Woo hoo," Hank Hardy turned his head and saw Jezabelle crossing the street. Hank reached Jezabelle at the same time Phoebe Harkins did.

"I thought I told you to stay in your house until we were done and we were sure it was safe," Hank chastised Jezabelle.

"It's okay, Mr. Hardy," said Phoebe, "she was coming to see me—weren't you, Jezabelle? She wanted to make sure I hadn't swooned my last swoon since I haven't been out all day." Phoebe placed a hand on Hank Hardy's arm and batted her long fake eyelashes in his direction.

Jezabelle began to reply, "Well, uh, uh, actually," holding up the pie, "I was going to uh…"

"My place." Phoebe grabbed the pie out of Jezabelle's hands and grabbed her arm propelling her towards her house. "I'll take good care of her, Chief Hardy!" Phoebe again batted her eyelashes in the direction of the police chief.

Jezabelle pulled away from Phoebe's grasp. "What are you doing, Phoebe? I was going to check on Mr. Warbler."

Phoebe answered, "No, you were going to Warbler's to snoop and find out why he was in Annabelle's backyard late last night."

"How did you know?" Jezabelle stopped and glared at Phoebe.

"Because I followed Miranda Covington. I always wondered where she went at night and so last night I followed her, although I haven't jogged in years and I was huffing and puffing just trying to keep up with her."

"What does that have to do with Warbler?" Jezabelle questioned.

Phoebe looked up. "We have to go."

"Go where?"

"They're looking at us. We have to go to my house so they won't be suspicious. Come on." Phoebe again grabbed Jezabelle by the arm and led her up the steps and into her house.

Once in the house, Phoebe grabbed the pie, took it into the kitchen, grabbed a fork, and began to eat the pie.

"That pie wasn't for you," Jezabelle reminded Phoebe. "It was for Mr. Warbler."

"Well, I have to make it look good in case they come to check on us."

Jezabelle shook her head. "Finish your story. How did you know Warbler was in Annabelle's backyard, and what does it have to do with you following Miranda Covington?"

"Miranda met Warbler." Phoebe gave Jezabelle a knowing look.

"No, she's too young for him." Jezabelle countered.

"Well, I don't know what they did. I had to leave because I was tired and I had to get my beauty sleep. How did you know Warbler was in Annabelle's backyard?"

"Well, uh, um, uh, I had company late last night and, after I locked up, I had a little glass of wine and sat out on my upstairs porch looking at the stars. I saw Warbler sneaking home at 2:00 a.m., but I didn't see Miranda." Jezabelle couldn't look Phoebe in the eyes.

"You had company? Who? Who? Who? Tell me. Tell me."

"Aren't wise old owls supposed to know everything? Who? Who?" Jezabelle mimicked Phoebe's tone. "Good bye, Phoebe." Jezabelle grabbed her pie pan and dashed out the door before Phoebe could stop her.

All eyes across the street at the crime scene turned as Phoebe shouted, "Thanks for the pie, you know who!"

CHAPTER SEVEN

The police and hearse left, but not before the police had stopped at each house in the neighborhood and warned the residents to let the officers know if they saw anything suspicious. Jezabelle noticed no one answered when the police knocked on Miranda's door or Rock's. It didn't surprise Jezabelle since Miranda never seemed to answer her door and, of course, Rock never came home until 10:00 p.m. Jezabelle could see the notices left on their doors before the police proceeded to the next block.

Darkness was descending. Jezabelle checked the time. It was almost 9:00 p.m. Mr. Warbler had not been out to feed his birds and squirrels at 8:00 p.m. *Had something happened to him again?* Grabbing her sweater to keep her warm from the cool spring air, Jezabelle grabbed another piece of pie, left her house, and went across the street to Mr. Warbler's house. Before knocking, she put her ear to the door. There was no sound coming from inside the house. She lifted her hand and touched the button for the doorbell, noticing the doorbell looked out of place on the old house. She could hear the doorbell chiming throughout the house.

"Come in—the door's open!" Mr. Warbler shouted.

Opening the door, Jezabelle first poked her head around to ogle the entryway. There was no one in sight. Juggling the piece of pie in one hand and closing the door with the other, Jezabelle moved her body farther into the house.

"Who is it?" Warbler queried from an unseen place.

"I'm stealing your silverware so I can't divulge that information," Jezabelle countered back with a muffled gruff voice.

"Jezabelle, quit playing tricks! I'm upstairs in the bedroom by the hole in my floor. Come on up but be careful. It's dark up here!"

Jezabelle frowned. "Well, turn on the lights!"

"No, I'm trying to think like the floornapper and the lights might disturb me," Warbler answered.

Jezabelle shook her head and switched on the flashlight on her cell phone. Balancing the pie with one hand and the flashlight in the other, she tentatively took a step up on the first step. Usually, at her age, she held onto the railings. She'd learned her lesson when she was chasing down her former cat, bless his dear departed soul, and missed a step in her basement, resulting in a broken leg and surgery that had laid her up for weeks. Her cat, Alabaster, had kept her company while she was on the mend. She didn't know if Alabaster was departed, but he had departed her house when she was well, following a little boy with crutches. Alabaster decided to live with the little boy. Although she missed Alabaster, when she saw the look on little Chris's face when he gazed at the cat, she had let Chris have Alabaster.

Since she couldn't hold onto the rails, she took her time climbing the wide steps that curved around to the upstairs' floor. Shining her flashlight ahead of her, she spied Mr. Warbler in the bedroom to the left. He was sitting next to the large hole in the floor.

"Here. I thought I'd feed you since you forgot to feed your birds." Jezabelle walked around the hole and handed the pie to her neighbor. "What are you really doing sitting here in the dark?"

Warbler mumbled, "I uh, wasn't kidding. I thought if I sat here I could tap into the mind of the person who stole this piece of floor."

"Did the fall bump your head so now you think you're a mind reader?"

"Who would do this and why? And why would they steal the same thing from Annabelle's house?" Mr. Warbler shook his head in confusion.

Jezabelle moved to the light switch, switching it on and illuminating the room. She studied the hole in the floor and walked the length of the bedroom peering down at the hardwood. "You know, my old house has a floor that has a square like this house did. The rest of the floor is normal hardwood just like this floor. Only the pattern of the hardwood is different. The same builder built all of the houses on this block. Eat your pie; you need to keep up your strength," Jezabelle ordered.

Warbler looked up at Jezabelle as he stuffed a bite from the pie into his mouth. In a garbled voice from his stuffed mouth, he asked, "Why steal a piece of floor, my floor?"

"And Annabelle's," Jezabelle reminded him. "Could it have something to do with your secret tryst with Miranda in Annabelle's garden?" Jezabelle's eyes twinkled at the question.

The pie Mr. Warbler was chewing on flew across the floor as he began coughing and choking. Jezabelle reached over and gave him a swift pat on the back.

Mr. Warbler pushed her hand away. "How did you know about that? Were you spying on me?"

With a smile, Jezabelle answered sweetly, "No, but Phoebe was spying on Miranda and I just happened to be having a nightcap on my second-story porch when you decided to call it a night. Phoebe was spying and I was gazing."

Mr. Warbler stood up and muttered something to himself and then raised his hand and slapped himself lightly on his forehead. "That's it! That's when they stole the piece of the floor. It was there before I left because I remember shaking the rug and putting it back by my bedside on the floor. I fell through the floor after I came back home."

"So why were you meeting Miranda?" Jezabelle asked again.

"Do you know this piece of floor had a picture carved into it with a small cross like a plus sign?" Mr. Warbler stared at the floor as though he was seeing the piece that had been stolen.

Jezabelle pointed her finger into Mr. Warbler's large chest. "You're changing the subject. Of course mine has a picture too, probably the same picture you had. I wonder if Annabelle had a drawing on her piece. I think mine is three ornate boxes. Was that what yours was?"

Silence greeted Jezabelle's question. Jezabelle grabbed the pie plate out of Warbler's hands. "Was—that—what—yours—was?" she asked again in a loud voice.

"Um... uh... I don't know," Mr. Warbler whispered.

Jezabelle leaned in. "What?"

"I...I... don't know."

Jezabelle threw her hands into the air. "How can you not know what your floor looks like? Didn't you ever get down on your hands and knees to clean it?"

Looking sheepish, Mr. Warbler hung his head. "Uh... uh... no."

Jezabelle's eyes opened wide. "You didn't clean your floor? It looks pretty clean to me." She looked around the room.

"I... uh... think the police cleaned it when they were done investigating," Warbler answered.

"I will phrase it a different way." Jezabelle was holding on to her temper. "Did you ever notice the pattern in the floor?"

Mr. Warbler's eyes shifted to the side of the room and he mushed his lips tightly together in thought. Shaking his head, he answered, "No."

Jezabelle was about to blast Mr. Warbler with some words that she didn't use very often when they heard the roar of a motor. It was Rock Stone pulling into his driveway and revving his engine twice. Instead of answering, Jezabelle walked to the window to watch Rock. Mr. Warbler joined her at the window.

Rock Stone got out of his car, gave a last puff on his cigarette before putting it out, then walked up to his door. He grabbed the note the police had left for him. Through the window and from their positions across the street, they heard Rock Stone break into a loud laugh before crumpling up the note, throwing it to the ground, and stepping into his house.

CHAPTER EIGHT

The next morning Jezabelle saw Mr. Warbler out in his yard feeding the birds and his squirrels. The squirrels were used to Mr. Warbler, and they followed him around his yard, chattering as if to scold him for missing a day of their feed.

Jezabelle stepped onto her porch enjoying the spring morning. Looking up and down her street, all seemed normal as if yesterday had never happened. The Brilliant Junk Company truck was pulling up to Miranda's to empty her trash. Quickly, Jezabelle stepped off her porch to get to her garage so she could put her garbage on the curb. With all the excitement of yesterday, she'd forgotten it was garbage day.

"Hi, Hick!" Jezabelle greeted Hickory Raferty as the garbage man pulled the truck up to Jezabelle's driveway.

"Just in time, Jezabelle! I thought you might have forgotten about me," Hickory teased, his eyes twinkling with mischief.

"Why, Hickory, how could I forget about a good lookin' fellow like you—makes my old heart beat double-time."

Hickory laughed; he and Jezabelle always flirted a little when he picked up her garbage. Though she was a senior citizen and he was in his middle thirties, they enjoyed their little joking flirtation. Jezabelle always told him if she couldn't flirt with the young guys, how was she going to catch an old guy. She would comment that she didn't want her flirting skills to get rusty and there weren't that many old guys around anymore to catch. They were either married or six feet under. "Practicing up, Jezabelle? Who's the lucky geezer now?"

"That's for me to know and you to never find out, Hick. Were you around yesterday? I thought I saw your truck."

"I drove through your neighborhood pretty early. Why do you ask? It's not my usual day." Hickory didn't look at Jezabelle when he answered, busying himself with dumping the trash.

Jezabelle laughed. "Oh, I see you haven't read the *Brilliant Times Chronicle* yet this morning. You might want to check it out. It's got the best picture of an old bird hanging out." Without waiting for an answer from Hickory, Jezabelle turned and walked back to her house and picked up her *Brilliant Times Chronicle* which was always waiting for her on her porch when she woke up in the morning. She could hear Hickory's truck continue down the street.

Her cell phone rang as she entered her house. "Delight, how nice of you to call. How are things in Fuchsia?"

"Here? What about there? I just heard the news; they found a body in your neighborhood!" Delight's loud voice reverberated through the phone.

"Just an accident, no need to worry," Jezabelle answered not wanting to upset her niece should she rush over to help. Delight and her friends always seemed to be in some trouble in Fuchsia, and she didn't need Delight bringing her friends and trouble to Brilliant. "I'd love to talk with you, dear, but I, uh, have an appointment at the, uh, Brilliant Library. We're going to rename it, and I want to

make sure I'm in on the decision. Toodles!"
Jezabelle quickly hung up the phone.

Staring at the paper in her hand, an idea began to form in her brain. Tossing the paper in the basket in the corner of her kitchen, Jezabelle grabbed her sweater and her purse and headed out the door locking it behind her.

CHAPTER NINE

When Molly Burnside opened her door, she heard Jezabelle muttering to herself before she saw her standing over to the side of the porch. "Jezabelle, what a surprise!"

"Hi, Molly, is Bart home?" Bart was Molly's teenaged son.

Molly frowned. "No, he's been gone this week with the high school marching band. It's their spring trip. Why do you need to see him?"

"Well, I don't know if you've heard, but my neighborhood has been victimized by a floornapper and I wondered if Bart saw anything when he was delivering yesterday morning's paper."

"Floornapper? Uh, I don't know what that is," Molly answered, confusion peppering her tone. "And you'll have to talk to Tom. He delivered the paper for our son yesterday. What's a floornapper?"

Jezabelle turned and walked down the steps away from Molly. "Got to go! I'll catch Tom at work. I'll give you a hint: a floor doesn't nap, such as in sleep. Get it?"

Molly rolled her eyes. "No, but I'll warn 'im, I mean, I'll let Tom know you're coming."

Jezabelle climbed into her Smart Passion Coupe that she'd just bought last week. Since she lived in Brilliant, which was smarter than the average community, she'd decided she should have her own Smart Car. It was just her size. Jezabelle always had a problem squeezing into a parking space. At times, she'd have to move the car forward with a few little bumps, and then move the car backward with a few taps to the bumper, but with her Smart Car, the car fit itself into the space just right. No more tapping and bumping, and no more lectures from HH about her driving.

Tom Burnside worked at Intellectual Icicles. The company made icicles that flashed different colors according to the temperature outside and alerted people to the weather. The colors also changed with the weather report. If it was warm and sunny, the icicles would flash back and forth between red, orange, and white. If it was going to be cloudy and snowy, they would flash blue and purple, and if it was very cold, they flashed silver. There were many different color combinations. The icicles were webbed into a unit that covered the entire roof of a house in the winter; this was connected to icicles hanging on the eaves. The web and icicles were then plugged in and warmed the roof and eaves. The snow would melt and the Intelligent Icicle wrap kept the water warm so it would flow down the spouts into a barrel at the bottom of the eave spouts. The disposable barrel would freeze and the city department would haul the barrel away each day, sometimes twice a day to the field coming into town. The haulers would peel the disposable wrapping off the ice, and the frozen barrels would line the roadway into Brilliant. Yes, sir, there was no snow on the rooftops of Brilliant, Minnesota, in the winter. The best part was the City of Brilliant paid the electricity bill for this feature.

Tom Burnside was inspecting one of the webbed sheets in the factory when Jezabelle found him. "Hi, Tom, you weren't in your office so I figured I'd find you here."

Tom looked up from the icicle he was inspecting. "Jezabelle, what can I help you with? Didn't I just sell you one of these last winter?"

"Yup, got pretty drippy at my house last winter. I understand you've been delivering my paper while Bart's been gone?"

"Oh, no! Did I forget to give you your paper?"

"No, but you may have heard we've had a little excitement on my street. I was wondering if you saw anything interesting day before yesterday when you were delivering in the early morning hours?"

"Well, Max was out and whining under Phoebe's window. I think he wanted Jasper to come out. It was still dark at 5:00 a.m., and there was a light on in Miranda Covington's house, which was unusual as her house is usually dark. You had a cat sitting on your porch. When did you get a cat? And... let's see... I thought I heard a loud thump at Annabelle's as I was walking by, but I figured it was the cat sitting on Annabelle's porch that could be a twin for your cat."

Jezabelle frowned. "I don't have a cat. I haven't seen a cat sitting on my front porch and there are two cats that look shifty? A thump? You must have heard Mr. Anonymous falling through the floor at Annabelle's. Are you sure you didn't see anything else?"

Tom shook his head. "No, sorry, maybe I should tell the police about the thump."

Jezabelle patted Tom on the hand. "No, you take care of your icicles and I'll take care of telling HH about the thump." Walking out the door of the factory, Jezabelle decided that she'd tell HH about the thump, but just not yet. She had to get the timeline down starting from the time Mr. Warbler was at Annabelle's and the time the perpetrator took the floor and knocked off the stranger. That meant she had to talk to Warbler again since he still hadn't told her what he was doing at Annabelle's in the middle of the night.

CHAPTER TEN

As Jezabelle pulled into her driveway, she saw Rock Stone pull up into his driveway at the same time. She couldn't remember when she'd last seen Rock at home at this time of day.

"Hey, Rock! What you doing home at this hour? You sick?" Jezabelle greeted him as she got out of her car.

"Oh... the... police... want to... question... me," he said in his slow drawl. "They... think... I... know... something..."

"Do you?" Jezabelle asked.

"I... know... I'm... out of... cigarettes." He laughed.

"How's your floor?" Jezabelle was curious to see if he knew about the floornapping. She'd never been in Rock Stone's old house. Maybe he didn't have the patterned floors like the rest of the neighbors did.

Rock frowned in confusion. "My floor? You... want to... know... about my... floor? Should... I... call a doctor? That's a... strange... question."

"Why do you think the police want to question you?"

"Ah... because... I... took... my pet... snake... to... church... with me... last... Sunday... night... and... Iggy... crawled... out of... my... pocket and... crawled... up the... Pastor's leg. He... got... scared, picked it up... and in... fear... threw it... out into... the... congregation... and it... landed...

on the... organist's... head. The... organist... freaked out and... knocked... Iggy... on top... of the... organ and Iggy... freaked out... too and... crawled... into a... pipe... in the... organ. They... had to... take the... organ... apart. Iggy... still... hasn't... recovered." Rock pulled a long snake out of his pocket to show Jezabelle. "Do you... want... to hold... him?"

Jezabelle lifted her hands and backed away from Rock. "No, maybe some other time. This conversation has taken up a lot of my time. Good luck with the police. But can I bring you some apple pie later? You can show me your floor."

Before Rock could answer, Jezabelle was sprinting up the front steps of her house and out of hearing distance.

Opening the door to her house, she felt something brush her leg and scoot past her. She looked down in time to see a huge, fluffy black and white cat hide under the couch. "Shifty, get out of here! I don't need a cat. You're so big; how can you fit in that little space? Go back to Annabelle's or go back to wherever you belong!" she ordered the cat.

The big fluff ball seemed not hear her, and a loud purr emanated from under the sofa.

"Fine, you can stay for a little while. But don't get in the habit of thinking I'm going to keep you," Jezabelle warned, sitting down on the floor next to the sofa.

She looked at her hardwood floor in her living room. *Nothing unusual about this floor*, she thought. The floor that was ornate with carvings was in her spare bedroom upstairs. Maybe she should check on it to make sure it was all there. She hadn't been in there for some time, not since Delight and Ella had come for a visit and stayed overnight so they could experiment with some recipes for Delight's restaurant, the Pink Percolator. They both liked to bake and, once or twice a year, Delight wanted to get out of Fuchsia so she would come stay with Jezabelle. They would bake up a storm of new concoctions for Delight's business.

Jezabelle stood up. She could see through her window that HH and Steve Stick had arrived to question Rock Stone. She chuckled. That was going to be a long interview. Looking down at the cat still under her couch, she decided to pop downtown to the Brilliant Bistro, get some lunch, and see what the gossip was.

There was no one outside at Rock Stone's anymore so Jezabelle assumed the police were inside questioning Rock and examining his floors. She waved to Mr. Warbler, who was in his yard puttering with his bird feeders. She reminded herself that she still had to find out what he was hiding.

CHAPTER ELEVEN

Jiffy greeted Jezabelle as she entered the Bistro. "I hear you make a mean pie, Jezabelle. Any chance you could make them for the Bistro? My baker didn't show up last week and everyone's complaining about my baking skills."

"Who told you about my pies? I only make them for special people. Like when I want them to spill their guts to me about something," Jezabelle whispered, "I don't want anyone to know about it. I have a secret ingredient that I put in the pie to make people talk."

Jiffy's eyes got as big as saucers. "Really? Ooh, we'd know everything that's going on in town if we had your pies. What's the ingredient?"

Jezabelle leaned closer. "It's a secret, patented by the CIA. If I told you, they'd have to do away with you, so don't tell anyone. Got that?" Jezabelle snapped her fingers in his face.

Before Jiffy could say anything, Jezabelle heard someone calling her name. Lizzy Langer was sitting at the corner table. She was Jezabelle's best friend and had been out of town. Jezabelle went to join her.

"What were you telling Jiffy Jacks?" Lizzy laughed. "If his eyes got any wider, they'd have popped."

"Did you tell Jiffy about my pies, Lizzy?"

"I did. They're too good to keep to yourself. You could have a new business going in your old age."

"When did you get back in town?" Jezabelle asked her old friend. "Did you hear about the floornapping and the dead person in Annabelle's house?"

Lizzy's eyes twinkled. "Well, I saw some of it on the front page of the *Brilliant Times Chronicle*. Has Warbler come after you yet for snapping that picture?"

Jezabelle leaned in to make sure no one at the tables around them could hear. "No, I think he's too worried about who and why someone stole his floor and... he has a secret that he doesn't want anyone to know."

Lizzy leaned closer and whispered, "What do you think it is?"

"I don't know, but he was seen sneaking around at Annabelle's the night his floor was taken and the night Mr. Anonymous fell through Annabelle's floor."

Lizzy gasped, "Someone died in Annabelle's house? I didn't hear that. You think Mr. Warbler killed him? I was always a little sweet on the guy, but I always thought he was sweet on you."

Jezabelle's head bobbed up and she peered at Lizzy. "What? Me? I don't think so."

"Who saw them?" Lizzy asked.

"Phoebe, of all people, and I did too when I was sitting on my upstairs porch at 2:00 am."

"You were sitting on your porch at 2:00 a.m. by yourself?" Lizzy gave Jezabelle a suspicious look.

"I can't look at the stars on my own porch in the middle of the night?"

"Jezabelle, you're hiding something too. Tell me."

Jezabelle gave Lizzy a sly look. "Nothing to tell yet. Let's get back to the subject—who was the dead guy and who's stealing our floors?"

A big crash from the kitchen interrupted their conversation. Smoke poured out of the oven and an off-color word was muttered by Jiffy Jacks.

Lizzy, holding in her laughter, looked at Jezabelle. "And you still don't want to help the poor guy out? If he keeps this up, with his baking he'll burn down the Bistro and then we can call it the Burning Bistro of Brilliant."

Jezabelle shushed Lizzy while pointing to the door. Hanna Hardy and Jeb Jardene had just walked in, looked around, and upon seeing Jiffy back in the kitchen, continued their journey through the Bistro and into the kitchen.

"What do you suppose is happening?" Lizzy whispered to Jezabelle.

"Jezabelle! Lizzy!" Phoebe Harkens called out as she sat down at their table.

"Where did you come from, Phoebe?" Jezabelle asked.

Phoebe leaned over and whispered to the two women, "The back door. I followed Hanna and Jeb over from Miranda Covington's house."

"What were they doing at Miranda's house? I didn't see them there. When I left I only saw HH and the Stick next door questioning Rock." Jezabelle questioned, waiting for Phoebe to continue talking.

"After you left, Hanna and Jeb pulled up to Miranda's house. It took Miranda a long time to open her door. They went inside for a few minutes, then Hanna walked across the street to Rock's house for a while and then Hank and Miranda talked outside. Then Jeb and Miranda went back inside Miranda's house and came out with Miranda and they all three got in the police car."

"Did they have Miranda handcuffed?" Lizzy asked.

"No, it didn't look like they'd arrested her, but then I've never seen someone arrested so they could have. Maybe they don't use handcuffs and cuff their hands behind their backs anymore. Do you know?" Phoebe looked back and forth between the two women to back up her statement.

"I have no idea," Jezabelle stated as she watched Jiffy, Hanna, and Jeb still talking in the kitchen. "How did you get from there to here? Miranda doesn't seem to be anywhere in the line of fire."

"No, they left her off at the police station. Well, they didn't leave her off. They all went in, and then after about fifteen minutes, Hanna and Jeb came out by themselves. No Miranda." Phoebe gave both women a wicked smile. "Aha! They did arrest her!"

Jezabelle looked up in time to see Miranda come through the front door of the Brilliant Bistro. "You can wipe that wicked look off your face. Miranda just walked in. And—why did you follow them, Phoebe?"

Phoebe had a sheepish look on her face. "I, ah, was bored and since Miranda had met Mr. Warbler I thought I'd follow her and see what she was up to. I didn't have anything better to do with my day. Life can get so boring when you're naturally beautiful and naturally rich." She gave a sigh.

Lizzy's ears perked up when she heard that Miranda had followed Mr. Warbler. "Miranda followed Mr. Warbler? Where? Tell me?" Lizzy grabbed Phoebe's arm.

Before Jezabelle could answer, Miranda Covington spied the three women and joined them at their table. Miranda's face was grim as she sank down onto a chair. Watching the conversation in the kitchen too, she commented, "Poor Mr. Jacks. To lose a baker but also a second cousin's cousin by way of marriage is hard."

The three women's mouths fell open at Miranda's statement. They looked at Miranda, looked at the three people in the kitchen, and all began to talk at once.

"What?" Jezabelle frowned.

"Second cousin's cousin by marriage?" Lizzy threw up her hands in confusion.

Phoebe was confused. "Where did he lose him? Do we need to go look for him?"

"No," Miranda explained. "The lost have been found. Found in the basement of Annabelle's house—dead."

"What?" Jezabelle screwed up her face in confusion, her wrinkles more prominent from the contortion. "I saw the dead body and I didn't know him. How did you know him?"

"Well, ya know I don't go out much during the day. I'm a writer. I guess I never told you that, but I also never told you that I moonlight a little and when Fred couldn't always be at the Brilliant Bistro to pop the goods in and out of the oven, I would jog downtown during the night and start the baking, or pop things out for him when they were done. We always communicated by texts, so I only met him once when he and I accidently got our texts crossed and we both showed up the week before Easter to put in the hot cross buns. I thought it was funny that our texts got crossed over hot cross buns." Miranda smiled at the memory.

Lizzy broke up the far-off look in Miranda's eyes. "Ok, earth to Miranda. How did they know to question you, and how did they make the connection?

Miranda sat up straight in her chair, squared her shoulders, and cleared her throat. "Well, Jiffy reported Fred missing this morning. But he didn't have a picture to show them. Who doesn't have a picture of his second cousin's cousin by marriage?" Miranda paused waiting for an answer.

Jezabelle, almost out of patience with the younger woman, sighed. "Get on with it."

"Well," Miranda continued, "Jiffy thought I might know something since I'm the backup oven-sticker so he gave the police my name. They asked if I had a picture and I did. I almost didn't answer the door because I was right in the middle of a murder scene for my new book, *The Pot Sticker*, when they came to my door and I didn't want to lose my train of thought."

Lizzy stood up quickly and impatiently tapped the table in front of Miranda. "Focus, Miranda, focus!"

Miranda sat up straighter and looked each of the three women in the eye. Phoebe having been quiet, gently said, "Go on, dear, we know this is hard for you."

Miranda cleared her throat again. "Well I did have a picture of him because I thought Fred was so cute I'd secretly snapped a picture of him when he was putting the hot cross buns in the oven. Did I tell you he had cute buns too?" Miranda giggled in memory.

"So how did he get in Annabelle's house and why is he dead?" Jezabelle raised her voice when asking the question, causing the rest of the patrons of the Bistro to turn in their direction.

Lizzy and Phoebe shushed Jezabelle at the same time. They were rewarded with a look only Jezabelle could get by with when she was annoyed.

"What were you and M—" A glass of water fell on Phoebe's lap just as she was going to ask Miranda about her rendezvous with Mr. Warbler at his house. Phoebe stood up sputtering, "Wha... What are you doing Jezabelle, trying to drown me?"

"I'm so sorry, Phoebe, but we must go. Come on, I'll drive you home so you can get some dry clothes." Winking at Lizzy, Jezabelle helped Phoebe up and out of the Bistro before Phoebe could protest.

Lizzy, knowing her best friend's tactics, winked back and turned to Miranda engaging her in conversation so Jezabelle could get Phoebe out of the building. She knew Jezabelle would explain herself later.

CHAPTER TWELVE

"What was that?" Phoebe asked on the drive home, still sputtering and complaining about her wet clothes. "I was going to ask her about her meeting with Mr. Warbler."

"I know. Why do you think I drowned you? We can't play our cards too soon. She and Warbler are up to something. They have a secret, and we can't let them know we're on to them," Jezabelle explained.

Phoebe frowned. "On to what? Maybe if we ask, they'll tell us. Maybe the police have already asked."

"No, because no one told the police about Mr. Warbler's strange behavior, did they?" Jezabelle asked Phoebe, making sure she hadn't spilled the beans.

"Well, no. I haven't talked to the police about that. Don't you think we should tell them?"

"It's probably not important." Wanting to change the subject so Phoebe didn't get any more ideas about contacting the police, Jezabelle asked, "Phoebe, does your floor have any designs on it? I can't remember."

"My sun room off to the side of my house does. It's an unusual floor. It has a pattern and one block of floor about the size that was stolen from Warbler's and Annabelle's."

"Does it have three ornate boxes on it?"

"No, it has more of a border design. It kind of reminds me of a hedge. And there's a small cross in the corner."

Jezabelle hesitated, deep in thought. "Does Miranda have the same type of floors we do?"

"Have you ever seen anyone enter Miranda's house except for the police?" Phoebe reminded her. "She really keeps to herself, but I guess now that we know she's a writer that would make sense. It probably explains her going out at night at odd times."

"It doesn't explain why she was at Annabelle's house with Warbler. He's too old for her," Jezabelle pondered.

"Well, maybe she's after his money," Phoebe suggested.

"Warbler has money? How do you know that?"

Phoebe blew on her nails. "Because, my dear, I'm beautiful and I have money, and I make it my business to know who else has money, especially in this neighborhood. He would have been a good catch for me had he been at least ten years younger and a hundred fifty pounds lighter. But the biggest problem for me is the birds. He'd never love me as much as he loves his birds. So *I* go after the fish. There's a lot of fish in the sea."

Phoebe flicked her hand in Jezebel's direction and got out of the car that Jezabelle had parked in front of Phoebe's house.

Jezabelle's head was still spinning when she drove her car into her garage. One never knew where Phoebe's mind was on any given day.

A vase of flowers waited for Jezebel when she stepped onto her porch. She picked it up and smelled the sweet smell of roses. A smile lit up her face as she read the card. Before she could put the card down, a hand came up over her shoulder and snatched it away. Jezabelle turned to see HH smirking at the greeting on the card.

"*The stars were bright for our little night, deep in the heart of Brilliant?*" Come on, Jezabelle, I could come up with something more romantic than that. Who's it from?" Hank Hardy's eyes twinkled as he asked.

Jezabelle snatched the card out of his hands. "You tried years ago, don't you remember? But then you decided the stars didn't twinkle anymore for me. What brings you here, HH?"

"We know the identity of the person found in Annabelle's house."

"I already know he's the second cousin's cousin by way of marriage to Jiffy." Jezabelle used her smug tone.

"Where did you hear that? Do I have a leak in my department?" Hank queried.

"I have my ways, Hank Hardy. Any idea whodunit?"

"I came here to examine your floors. I checked out Rock Stone's earlier today," Hank informed her.

Jezabelle laughed as she opened the door and motioned Hank inside. "Long conversation?"

Hank looked confused. "Huh?"

Jezabelle raised her eyes. "Never mind—the floor's this way upstairs." Jezabelle led the way up. She stood back and let Hank enter the room first.

Hank walked around the room, slowly examining the floor while Jezabelle watched. He got down on his knees and ran his fingers over the piece of floor that had the three ornate boxes design. After tapping around the square of wood, he looked up at Jezabelle. "I suspect if we pulled this part of the design up, we would find the floor and joists were built the same way. This was framed in a square where the rest of the floor is framed as a usual floor. Do you have any idea of the history of this house?"

"I know it was built by the Brilliant Brothers after they founded Fuchsia, but I've only lived here since my mid-twenties, but you know that. I bought the house after I decided I didn't need an HH in my life. Or should I say, you didn't need a Jezzy in your life."

Hank ignored the sarcasm in her voice. "These houses are all well kept and they all have their original features except for Warbler's modern-looking doorbell and button."

Jezabelle shook her head in agreement. "Isn't that an eyesore. I should get the historical society on him about that. It must violate some historical code."

Hank stood up. "Until we figure out what's going on, you and your neighbors need to be careful. This seems to be the only neighborhood they are targeting. I'm going to make sure we add more patrols to the block." He turned and walked into the hallway and toward the stairs.

Jezabelle followed. "We'll put Max and Jasper on guard. I'll warn Warbler and the other neighbors."

"No need—while I was here I had Jeb and Hanna warn the others."

"Did you check the floors in their houses too, Hank?"

Hank stopped at the door and turned. "We did. All have a different design than you and all are built the same, but why someone would steal them has us baffled."

Hank opened the door and was almost knocked over by a large fluffy black and white cat as it dashed into the house. "Jezzy?"

Jezabelle shook her head in exasperation. "I didn't—the cat got me. It's the cat that kept sneaking into Annabelle's house. I call him Mr. Shifty because he wants to be a cat burglar. He seems to think I belong to him."

"Maybe you should adopt him."

"No! No more cats. It hurts too much to lose them and after Alabaster left to go live with Chris, I decided no more animals." Jezabelle sniffed, remembering Alabaster.

Stepping outside, Hank laughed. "Well, I think Mr. Shifty has stolen something else and has decided to stash it here too." Hank pointed to a cat, an exact duplicate of the one that had dashed into her house.

The cat eyed Jezabelle and then eyed Hank and then, faster than you could say catnip, it dashed through Jezabelle's door and joined Mr. Shifty under the couch.

Hank suggested, "You could use them as guard cats." He shut the door firmly and Jezabelle could hear his laughter as he proceeded to his squad car.

CHAPTER THIRTEEN

Jezabelle was taking her chocolate peanut butter cup cheesecake out of the oven when she heard her old-fashioned doorbell ring. *What now?*

Rock Stone stood on her doorstep. "I... need... your help."

"Well, Rock, what can I help you with and why are you still home?"

"I... took the night shift... so I could... take today... to... talk to the... police."

Jezabelle sighed. "You might as well come in, Rock, I can see this is going to take awhile." She motioned him into the house then into the kitchen. "I was just finishing up my cheesecake."

Rock stared at the cheesecake. "That... is... why... I needed... to... talk to... you. I am... supposed... to... bring... dessert to... work. It is... my... birthday... and I am... supposed... to... bring... the birthday... treat. Fred... Rally... was supposed... to... bake... me a... cake... but I... just... found... out he's... dead... and I... have... no cake." He eyed the cheesecake.

"You knew dead Fred?" Jezabelle asked. "Why have I never heard of him before or seen him? How did you know him?" She gently moved her cheesecake out of sight behind her body.

"He... was... my best... friend... in high... school. He... was... quiet. He... didn't want... to... be... out in... public... much. He only... came...

out at... night. He... didn't... like the... sunshine. Said... it hurt... his... skin."

"Do you know why he was in Annabelle's house?" Jezabelle watched her neighbor closely for any signs he might be lying.

"No... He said... he... was... going... to go to... the... Bistro... and bake my... cake. Can... I... buy... your... cheesecake?" Rock looked around Jezabelle's body at the cooling cheesecake.

Jezabelle was silent for a moment but when she looked into Rock's eyes, she saw the eyes of a man looking like he was drowning. "No, you can't buy it, but you can have it. It needs to cool a little longer and then it needs to come out of the springform pan. Can you handle that or do you want to pick it up later?"

Relief showed in Rock's eyes. "I... can... handle... that. Thank... you. I know... you... are... a... little... nosy but... here's... the... spare key... to my... house. I... know... you are... dying... to... look at... my floor."

Jezabelle exchanged the cheesecake for the key. "Strange way to put it but yes, yes, I want to look at your floor for um... ah... historical purposes."

Rock laughed. Jezabelle led him to the front door and held it open for him so he wouldn't drop the cheesecake.

"Nice... cats... you have... there." Rock nodded at the cats still under the couch. "You... might... want... to keep... them... in so... nothing... happens... to them." Again he laughed as he exited out the door.

Jezabelle looked at the cats underneath the couch. "Did that sound like a threat to you?"

Both cats answered at the same time, "Meroow!!!!"

CHAPTER FOURTEEN

When Jezabelle woke the next morning, the first thing she did was check to see if her patterned floor was still there. She'd dreamed a ghostly presence had lifted the floor and floated out of the house through the walls with the piece of floor following the mysterious ghost. It seemed so real that it wasn't until Jezabelle checked her floor and had her first cup of coffee for the day that she let go of her dream. She noted the coffee hit the spot. She'd purchased it and brought it back from her trip to the Interchange in Albert Lea.

Mr. Shifty and the other cat, still in the house, were sitting on the window seat below the front window, peering out into the street. Mr. Shifty jumped up. The hair on his back stood straight up and he let loose with a loud yowl, scaring his look-alike so much that she fell off the bench. Jezabelle laughed and got up to see what was happening outside that had got Mr. Shifty so riled. It was Jasper and Max cavorting on her lawn. She opened her front door so the cats could join in the fun or go out and hiss at the dogs.

Watching the cats run out the front door, she decided maybe she should take the two cats to Dr. Dogwood at the Catniption Barkery and check to see if Mr. Shifty was really a mister and if the other cat was really a missus. Jezabelle, in her mind, had labeled them that way, but it could be a falsehood she needed to correct since it looked like she might be stuck with them.

Outside, Jezabelle saw Phoebe and Mr. Warbler leave their houses and go to their garages. All the garages in the neighborhood were in the back of the houses at the back of the large yards. It dawned on Jezabelle that she needed to get it together. She remembered that there was a meeting at the Brilliant Library, and she was sure that that was where Warbler and Phoebe were going. They were both active members of the Brilliant Library. The community was going to discuss renaming the library. It was such a beautiful old building and the library board thought the name should reflect its beauty. Although Brilliant was a fine name, everything in Brilliant that had been built by the Brilliant brothers was named Brilliant. It might be time for a change.

Dressing up in her finest, Jezabelle grabbed her purse, locked the door, and proceeded to her garage. On the way, she noticed that her ladder was lying in her yard. She usually kept it in the garage. Jonathon Piffle must have forgotten to put it away when he washed her windows earlier in the week. In the spring, Jonathan washed all the windows of all the Victorian houses on the street. It was easier to hire Jonathan than to try to climb the ladder herself.

The cats and dogs were still having a standoff in her front yard. She chuckled, thinking she'd put her money on the cats any day. The sun was shining through the trees lining the streets of Brilliant, highlighting the thoughtful planning the Brilliant brothers had brought to the community. The old trees stood tall and majestic, and she never failed to admire their beauty.

The parking lot of the library was full when she arrived, so Jezabelle pulled her car into the Brilliant Bank's parking lot. The bank didn't mind if library patrons used their lot. When the brilliant minds of Brilliant built the bank, they anticipated the spillover parking from the library. There hadn't been enough room on the other side of the street to have an expanded parking lot.

Sprinting across the street and up the steps of the library, Jezabelle noted that the clock outside the library was striking ten o'clock. She was just in time. There was an empty chair in the back of the meeting room so she slipped in unnoticed.

"Before we get on to the business of whether or not we want to rename the library, Hank Hardy wants to speak to us." Marian Markowsky, the librarian, nodded at Hank who'd been standing unnoticed in the back of the room.

"Many of you may have heard that there have been some thefts of pieces of floor in the Penderghast neighborhood. For those of you who are new to this community, that's the neighborhood that borders our community to the north where Mr. Warbler, Jezabelle Jingle, Rock Stone, Phoebe Harkins, and Miranda Covington live. You might also have heard that a dead body was found at Annabelle Avary's house. The victim's name was Fred Rally. He was a recluse and a baker at the Brilliant Bistro. Last night someone broke into the Brilliant Library and stole the original plat map of Brilliant that had been carved into the east wall of the Brilliant Brothers' Memorial Room. They cut it right out of the wall. We ask all citizens to be watchful for any strangers or any unusual behavior. Make a note that there will be a security system installed in this library now. Thank you." Hank nodded to Marion that she could take over the meeting.

Marion stepped forward and had to shout above the crowd a few times to quiet the din in the room created by Hank's announcement.

"Now to business at hand—but we need to add another item. Now that part of the wall has been knocked out in the Brilliant Brothers' Memorial Room, we need to decide if we might want to remodel some things along with changing the name of the library." Marion's eyes scanned the room to see how the meeting goers were taking her announcement.

"First you want to change the name of the library and then you want to change the name of a memorial room? What's wrong with it as it is? If it ain't broke, don't fix it!" Roland Door stomped his foot as he stood up to make his statement.

"But our library is so much more than just the name *Brilliant*. We have brilliant minds in our community, but it's the books and the learning that makes them brilliant, and I feel the name of the library should reflect the creativity of those minds," Molly Burnside softly suggested.

"Who would steal a plat map?" Jonathan Piffle asked.

"Jonathan, did you leave my ladder out when you washed my windows this week?" Jezabelle shouted from across the room.

"Who's going to bake the cakes for the Fireman's Dinner if Fred is dead?" Jet Pillager piped in.

"What about The Library of Lackadaisical Meanderings?" Lizzy suggested, rushing late into the room.

Phoebe, seeing that Marion was having a hard time controlling the meeting, stood up and let out a loud whistle. All eyes turned toward her. "Now that you're all quiet, may I suggest that you take your questions to the appropriate sources and not interrupt this meeting. As for the name of the library, may I suggest since I am rich that I offer a solution. We will have a contest for the renaming of the Brilliant Library. I will offer up five thousand dollars to the winner. The only stipulation is that I choose the winning name."

Silence greeted her suggestion. Jezabelle caught Lizzy's eye. Lizzy nodded and stood up. "I suggest we accept Phoebe's generous proposal but with one minor adjustment. Phoebe chooses five finalist names and then a committee from the community votes on the final winner. Would that be fair, Phoebe? Jezabelle and I will help you."

"I propose we accept Lizzy's proposal." Jiffy Jacks stood up.

Phoebe looked around the room, giggled, and said, "I guess I can give up my money for that proposal. I have one more stipulation though, and that is that my name is placed on the bottom of the plaque when it goes on the library. It should say, *Donated by Phoebe Harkins*."

Meekly, Marion suggested, "Do I hear a second that we have a contest, Phoebe Harkins donates the money, we committee members will all vote on the five best names chosen by Phoebe, and Phoebe's name will be placed underneath the winning library name because of her donation?" She sighed.

The word *second* rebounded around the room.

"Fine, now what about the hole in the wall?"

Jezabelle giggled. "That reminds me of the Hole in the Wall Gang. Let's just make it perfectly round and call it the *Hole in the Wall*. A little play on words."

The group chuckled and murmurs filled the room. "I like that idea," Mr. Warbler agreed. "We need to throw in a little humor because all those brilliant minds were *so* serious. I make that a motion!"

"I second it!" Phoebe chimed in.

"All in favor, say aye!" said Marion. The committee members all voiced their assent.

"Then, if there's no more business, we are adjourned. I will contact the carpenter once the police release the crime scene." Marion dismissed the group.

Jezabelle, Lizzy, Phoebe, and Mr. Warbler grouped together at the back of the room. "What do you suppose the plat map of Brilliant has to do with the burglaries and murder in our neighborhood?" Jezabelle asked the group.

Phoebe's eyes twinkled with excitement. "Ooh, it's like a treasure hunt."

Jezabelle stood up straight. "You're right, Phoebe. Come on!"

Phoebe's face lit up. "I am?"

"Where are we going?" Lizzie asked.

"To our neighborhood. Get your cars and meet at my house," Jezabelle instructed.

Hank Hardy joined the group. "And what are you all up to?" he asked, suspicious of their whispering.

"Just planning a spring party, Hank Hardy." Phoebe sauntered up to Hank and grabbed his arm, fluttered her fake eyelashes, and almost purred, "My what muscles you have, Hank. Would you like to stop over later and question me?"

Jezabelle and Lizzy grabbed Phoebe away from Hank. "We've got to go—the party's soon. We'll make sure you get an invite."

Mr. Warbler shrugged his shoulders and shook his head. "They're women; don't even try to figure them out."

"Phoebe, what was that?" Jezabelle asked as they led Phoebe to her car.

"What?" Phoebe faked innocence. "I got him off the trail of what we're doing and he is cute, and I kind of like him even if he is twenty-some years older than me. He can be the cougar to my black cat. Meow!" Phoebe used her fingers like fangs.

Jezabelle and Lizzy rolled their eyes.

"Home, Phoebe." Lizzy ordered.

CHAPTER FIFTEEN

The four friends gathered in Jezabelle's living room. "Phoebe, you're right. We need to put the pieces of the puzzle together."

"Start from the beginning," Lizzy instructed. "I don't live in this neighborhood and I was out of town so I'm kind of out of the loop."

"First, I fell through the floor when someone stole a piece of my floor." Mr. Warbler put the first piece of information out there.

"Then someone stole a piece of Annabelle's floor and poor Fred was dead," Phoebe continued.

"And now the plat map is missing from the library," Jezabelle added.

Lizzy was quiet for a moment. "What was on the pieces of flooring that were stolen?"

"Well, we don't know what was on Annabelle's since none of us saw it," Jezabelle answered.

"And ah, ah, I don't know…," Mr. Warbler muttered.

Lizzy frowned. "You don't know?"

"You don't know?" Phoebe echoed Lizzy's question.

Mr. Warbler lowered his eyes to the ground. "Well, uh, I remember there was a small cross in the corner."

"You don't know!" Phoebe's loud voice echoed in the room. "Don't you scrub your floors?"

Silence greeted her question, and Mr. Warbler looked at Jezabelle.

"That's neither here nor there. What do we have? Nothing."

The foursome sat in silence. Suddenly, they heard scratching at the door. Jezabelle got up and opened the door. Max, Jasper, Mr. Shifty, and the other cat entered the room.

"Who are those two cat creatures?" Mr. Warbler asked. "And what are they doing with Max and Jasper? Max and Jasper don't like cats."

"Did you get another cat and not tell me, Jezabelle?" Lizzy chided her friend.

"Well," Phoebe's haughty tone filled the room. "She didn't tell me either, and I live across the street. She let me think they were stray cats. How could you? I needed time to let Jasper adjust to a cat in the neighborhood."

Disgusted at the turn of the conversation, Jezabelle turned to Phoebe. "Don't you think it's time you renamed Jasper *Jasperine* since *he* is a *she*?"

Phoebe gasped and stood up at the taunt.

Lizzy stood up too. "We're getting off the subject. Treasure hunt? Remember?"

A clang sounded on the floor as something metal hit the coffee table. Max had batted a key at Mr. Shifty and Mr. Shifty had batted the key toward the other cat.

"That's it!" Jezabelle declared picking up the key. "The piece to the puzzle. Let's go see what the other pieces have on them. We can start at Rock's since I already know what's on mine—three ornate boxes. Rock gave me the key." Jezabelle opened the door and ushered her friends out of the house.

"We'll go in his back door. That's what the key is for," Jezabelle stated.

"I see Jonathan Piffle must have been here to wash your windows," Lizzy said noticing the ladder propped against the side of Jezabelle's house.

Jezabelle, not looking toward the ladder but referring to the ladder she'd seen earlier lying in her yard, answered, "He must have been and he didn't put my ladder away."

Opening Rock Stone's back door, Jezabelle hollered, "You hoo, Rock! Are you here?" Silence greeted her call. "He must be back on day shift. Worked all last night and must have stayed on today."

Jezabelle led the way upstairs to the room that Rock had said held the patterned floor.

Mr. Warbler looked around the room. "Look. Even the rest of his floor is different than our houses."

The four stood looking down at the piece of the floor that was different and square.

"It's words." Phoebe shook her head. "Words, not a picture."

"Faith, hope, charity," Jezabelle nodded. "Beautiful words, but what do they have to do with the picture?"

"And look! There's a small cross in the corner here too!" Warbler pointed out.

"Phoebe, you've never said what's on your floor," Lizzy said.

Phoebe shrugged her shoulders. "Some curlicue stuff. Around the border—or leafy; it's just a cute design."

"Are you sure?" Jezabelle questioned.

"All my floors are hardwood. I haven't seen one with a square like this—mine is different. Come and see."

Phoebe started down the stairs and indicated that the others should follow her.

As they were crossing the street, Miranda Covington stuck her head out of her upstairs window. "What are you all doing? It looks like you are mimicking the Beatles crossing Abby Road."

"Putting the pieces of a puzzle together. Do you want to join us?" Jezabelle hollered so Miranda could hear her.

"No, thanks! I'm in the middle of murdering someone. See you later!" Miranda closed her window and shrunk out of sight.

"Do you suppose we should take that literally?" Lizzy poked Jezabelle jokingly.

Once in Phoebe's house, she led them to the room she'd mentioned. "See, curlicues in this square."

Jezabelle studied the floors. "You're right. But the patterns in your entire floor are different too. Do you suppose that means something?"

Mr. Warbler, standing by the window, turned his head to look outside. "Ah, Jezabelle, you might want to go home."

Jezabelle turned to look at Warbler. "Why?"

"Ah, there are police cars surrounding your house." Warbler pointed out the window.

Jezabelle moved to the window. "My house is being arrested!"

CHAPTER SIXTEEN

"Hank Hardy, what are you doing arresting my house?" Jezabelle hollered across the street.

"Jezzy, are you okay?" Hank met her in the middle of the street.

"I'm fine; why?"

"We received a call saying there had been a burglary at your house, and all cars were needed."

"I was just at my house. It was fine."

Hank led her over to her house as Hanna and Jeb Jardene were exiting Jezabelle's house. "The floornapper's been at it again," Jeb informed Hank.

"What? And how did you get into my house?" Jezabelle asked. "We were just there. My floor wasn't missing."

Mr. Warbler, Lizzy, and Phoebe joined Jezabelle and the police in front of Jezabelle's house. "Is everything okay?" Lizzy asked, concerned.

"Apparently someone stole my floor."

"Your door was unlocked, Jezabelle. Didn't I tell you to keep your doors locked when you were gone? The time of unlocked doors in Brilliant is going to have to be over," Hank admonished.

"I locked my door." Turning to her friends, "Didn't I?"

"She did; I saw her," Lizzy stated.

"She did," Phoebe chimed in.

"I double checked," Mr. Warbler assured the group.

"Wait!" Lizzy said, walking to the back of the house. "The ladder's gone!"

Jezabelle and the others had followed Lizzy. "It is," said Jezabelle. "It was right here in the middle of the yard this morning. I was upset that Jonathan Piffle had left it out when he washed my windows."

"No," Lizzy countered. "Don't you remember when we went to visit Rock Stone, the ladder was propped on the side of your house by a window?"

Jezabelle frowned. "I thought you were talking about it being in the middle of the yard."

Hanna jumped in. "The perpetrator must have climbed in the window, removed the piece of the floor, and left by the open front door and no one saw him."

"He must have been watching us," Jezabelle surmised. "We went in the backyard and then he went out the front door. Do you suppose he was upstairs in the house when we were having our meeting?"

"But who called the police? It wasn't any of us," Mr. Warbler noted.

Jezabelle questioned Hank, "Who called?"

Hank shook his head. "Someone called from a cell phone and wouldn't leave their name. We couldn't tell by the voice if it was a man or a woman."

"I'll canvas the neighborhood and see if anyone else is home who could have called us." Jeb turned and walked toward Rock Stone's house.

"He's not home," Jezabelle told Hank.

"How do you know that?" Hank asked.

"He works the day shift, but last night he worked the night shift and stayed for the day shift. He took one of my cheesecakes to work with him and I saw him right before he left," Jezabelle explained.

"Well, maybe he's back home now and he's the one who called," Hank guessed.

"He's not!" Mr. Warbler, Lizzy, and Phoebe all answered at the same time."

Hank turned to the three. "And you know this how? What have you been up to?" At this last question, he turned and looked Jezabelle in the eye. "Jezzy?"

"We're working on a puzzle." A stubborn look formed on her face. "We're investigating the theft of the floors and the library wall. We're calling ourselves the Puzzle Professors. We know about puzzles."

"Yes, we're puzzled experts," Lizzy chimed in.

"You are that—puzzled," Hank agreed.

Phoebe sidled up next to Hank, batted her eyelashes, leaned in, and whispered in his ear, "You're not alone; the Puzzle Professors will help you solve this crime and it won't cost you a dime."

Hank quickly moved out of Phoebe's reach. "You need to stay out of this. Puzzle Professors? Jezzy, do you hear me?"

Hanna broke into the conversation. "You need to listen to Dad. I think there's more than one person doing this. They have to be working as a team to be able to get a piece of floor as large as the ones that have been stolen and also that large map out of the library building. They also put away your ladder. It's back hanging in your garage. One person couldn't have done all that alone in the short amount of time they had."

The group, concentrating on figuring out what was happening, didn't notice the car parked across the street flashing pictures of the group. The occupant yelled out the car window, "I need a scoop! I heard that the floornapper has struck again!

Say cheese!" Snoop Steckle snapped another picture as everyone in the group looked up to see who was yelling at them.

"Snoop Steckle, put that camera down! No pictures! We don't want to alarm the good citizens of Brilliant any more than they are," Hanna Hardy yelled back.

"Sweet Hanna, why don't we talk about it over dinner tonight? Perhaps you can give me the scoop so I don't have to snoop. We can dance till dawn and the night won't be a total yawn." Snoop laughed at the blush that was rising up Hanna's face.

"Meet me at the station, Snoop. I'll give you your scoop. Hanna's on duty tonight," Hank instructed.

Hanna frowned. "I am?"

"Yes, you are," her father answered firmly.

Jezabelle looked at the watch on her arm. "Are you done here? I have some baking to do. And I'm expecting something tonight."

Lizzy gave Jezabelle a pointed look. "Expecting something or someone?"

All eyes were on Jezabelle waiting for her to answer.

Before she could think of something to say, Jeb walked up to the group. "No one else home."

"Are you sure? Miranda Covington just hung out of her window an hour or so ago and she never goes out during the day," Jezabelle informed the cops.

"We're done here. You can get back to whatever it was you were doing. And I have just disbanded the Puzzle Professors, understand? It's too dangerous for you all to get involved." Hank motioned for his people to follow him.

The group watched as the police drove away.

Jezabelle made sure they were gone before turning to her friends. "Well, he may have disbanded the Puzzle Professors, but he didn't disband the Penderghast Puzzle *Protectors,* did he?" With a sly grin on her face, she continued, "New name! New game! Let's meet at the library, tomorrow morning at 10:00 a.m. in the Brilliant Brothers Room so we can investigate that crime scene and, if anyone asks why we're there, we decided to put a puzzle together. Oh, someone bring a real puzzle just to throw them off our game."

CHAPTER SEVENTEEN

Jezabelle held her glass of wine to her lips. It had been a beautiful night. She knew she should get to bed but it was so beautiful sitting on her upstairs porch watching the stars. Mr. Shifty and the other cat sat next to her purring loudly, content to be with their newly adopted mother.

She was about to turn in for the night when she noticed a strange light coming from Annabelle's house. At the same time as she noticed the light, she saw Miranda Covington run down her front steps, turn to the left, and continue on down the street out of sight. Jezabelle wondered if she was on her way to the Brilliant Bistro to help with the baking. That couldn't be it. Jezabelle knew Jiffy had made other arrangements.

While she was pondering Miranda's run, she saw Mr. Warbler sneaking out from behind Annabelle's house and across the street to his house. The moonlight cast a perfect light so Jezabelle could see his shadow as he wasn't using a flashlight. *What was Warbler up to?*

Jezabelle decided not to surprise Warbler by letting him know she was watching him from her upstairs porch. She wondered if it had anything to do with his missing floor. Or was he up to something else since he didn't seem to want to be seen. Jezabelle looked back over to Annabelle's house. All was quiet and dark. Did Warbler have a key to Annabelle's house?

Mr. Warbler had just entered his residence when Miranda came jogging back home. She stopped and gazed at Annabelle's before entering her own.

As Jezabelle was about to step back into her house, she noticed the light go on in Rock Stone's living room. She decided to pour herself another glass of wine and stay on her porch a little longer. Maybe Rock had some secrets too.

A car drove onto Rock's driveway and up to his garage. The woman in the car got out and lifted the garage door, since it didn't have an electric opener, got back in the car, and drove inside the garage. Jezabelle watched as the woman quietly knocked on Rock's door. The door opened and the woman joined Rock in the house. Jezabelle thought the dark shape of the woman looked familiar, but she couldn't make out exactly who it was in the darkness. The lights in Rock's kitchen went out and Jezabelle saw the soft glow of the television and no other lights coming through the living room window.

Jezabelle took a sip of wine. She needed to get to bed since they had to meet at the library in the morning. Phoebe seemed to be the only person sleeping this night. Jezabelle glanced at Phoebe's house. Phoebe was a strange character. In her mid-forties, she had married once but said her ex-husband was too in love with his mother to pay much attention to her. Phoebe never said how she acquired her wealth and, though she flaunted the fact in front of everyone, she had a heart of gold underneath the glamorous and at times haughty exterior. She occasionally appeared to be ditsy but her roots were in Brilliant, so she also had a brilliant mind. Phoebe's mother lived just down the block on the next street with Phoebe's sister.

It appeared all her neighbors had settled in for the night. Taking one more glance at Miranda's house, Jezabelle decided it was time for some shut-eye. Maybe they should call Miranda and invite her to the meeting. After all, writers had to keep secrets, didn't they? Jezabelle would ask the group in the morning if they wanted to include Miranda. She made one last toast to her neighborhood, then went into her bedroom and locked the door behind her.

CHAPTER EIGHTEEN

The Brilliant Library was empty of other people when the newly formed Penderghast Puzzle Protectors met in the Brilliant Brothers' Room. The gaping hole still was a gaping hole, waiting to be made into a finished gaping hole called the Hole in the Wall.

"I brought a puzzle for us to put together," Phoebe announced in a loud voice so it could be heard throughout the library.

Lizzy wrinkled her nose. "That's a five-thousand-piece puzzle! Are you nuts? We'll never put that together."

"That's the idea, Lizzy. It'll take us time so we can keep meeting here and no one will suspect." Phoebe gave Lizzy a scathing look.

"Look! It has birds and squirrels and butterflies. Oh, I love this puzzle already!" Mr. Warbler rubbed his hands together in excitement.

"Well, folks, what's happening here?" Marion, the librarian, eyed the puzzle. "Good to see you here so early. I've always questioned whether we should open this early because we're never busy until the afternoon."

Jezabelle cleared her throat. "We're the newly put together Penderghast Puzzle Protectors. We're protecting the extinction of puzzles, so we're also promoting solving puzzles."

Marion pondered the statement before answering, "Hmm, I didn't know puzzles were becoming extinct. I must be out of the loop. I spend too much time here. Can anyone join?"

"Well, uh, until we figure out if we can figure out a puzzle, we're limiting membership to the Penderghast neighborhood. Once we have the rules and regulations set, we may open it up," Phoebe answered.

"Yes, after all, you can't lead if you haven't followed," Jezabelle stated.

"Huh?" Her friends looked at each other and shook their heads.

"Well, carry on and good luck! I'll put you down for this room. Just let me know how often you need it, although not many people use it anyway. We all know the Brilliant Brothers' history already." Marion gave a slight wave as she left the group.

"Now what?" Lizzy asked.

Jezabelle plopped a book on the table. "This is a plat book. Granted, it's from this year but maybe by studying it we can figure out why they would steal the wall with the plat carving."

Frowning, Mr. Warbler asked, "Wouldn't there have been a book from back then? Why didn't they steal the book instead of the wall?"

Phoebe paged through the book. "Well, for one thing, back then I would imagine what was on the wall was the original farms around here, and I don't think there were probably as many as there are now or, at least, homesteads. And our community wasn't very big then because it was just founded, so I would imagine what was on the wall is very different than what we have today."

Jezabelle was always amazed when something serious and not flirtatious came out of Phoebe's mouth. "Let's ask Marion."

"Marion!" they all hollered at the same time.

Marion rushed back into the room with a finger over her lips. "This is a library," she whispered. "If you can't all abide by the quietness rules, your Penderghast Puzzle Protector Group will have to meet elsewhere."

"Marion, are there any plat books from when Brilliant was founded that have in them the map on the wall that was stolen?" Mr. Warbler asked.

Marion shook her head. "No, for some reason, the Brilliant Brothers only wanted it on the wall. They wouldn't allow that original plat to be printed. It's in the bylaws of the community."

"Really?" Jezabelle turned her back to Marion and mouthed to the group, "I have an idea."

"Thanks, Marion, and we promise we'll be quiet." Lizzy led Marion out of the room.

Warbler turned to Jezabelle and asked, "What?"

"Think about it. Our neighborhood—the Penderghast neighborhood—was on that plat map because our houses are the original houses. The Brilliant Brothers lived in our houses. There were seven brothers. Each one had a house. We know that. Our houses and this plat map are the only things that have been heisted in Brilliant. Maybe it *is* a puzzle."

"The brothers must have had a sense of humor even in their brilliance. What if they put together their houses like a puzzle? What could they have been hiding?" Lizzy wondered.

"Right," Jezabelle agreed. "And the answer is in our floors."

"Someone else must know too and apparently they're willing to kill for it. But why kill Fred Rally?" Mr. Warbler put the question to the group.

"Maybe he found something out by accident. What do we really know about him?" Jezabelle countered.

Phoebe's face lit up. "I can ask Hank. I'll sweet-talk him into telling me what he knows. Jezabelle, will you make me a gooey fudge chocolate tart and I'll have him over and offer him some whipped cream."

Jezabelle raised her eyebrows. "First things first, Phoebe. Hold on to those claws. We need to investigate what's left of the floors. Maybe because of the way they were framed in, the floors are actually being lifted up because there's also something hidden underneath the piece."

"How do we do that? The only floors left are Phoebe's, Miranda's, and Rock's. You think Miranda and Rock are going to let us cut up their floors?" Lizzy threw her hands in the air.

"Well, I have Rock's house key. We could do it while he's gone," Jezabelle suggested.

Phoebe's eyes opened wide. "Yah and he calls Hank because we stole his floor. Hank arrests us, and then he'll never accept my invitation for my chocolate tart."

"*My* chocolate tart, you mean," Jezabelle reminded her. "Here's an idea. Let's just talk to the other home owners and be honest. Tell them about our puzzle group and ask them to join and tell them we found out there's a treasure underneath their pieces of floor and then we put all the pieces together."

The group eyed Jezabelle for a moment before Mr. Warbler said, "But... we don't know there *is* treasure underneath their floor."

"Well, we don't know there *isn't*," Jezabelle reminded him.

"Good plan, meeting adjourned!" Phoebe moved to the door.

"Hold on, Phoebe! Everyone thinks we're a real puzzle group. Let's see if we can get the birds and butterflies to match up so no one gets suspicious," Lizzy reminded them.

"Right, we'll do a little of the puzzle each week until we get the real caper solved." Mr. Warbler sat down. "I've got this butterfly figured out!"

CHAPTER NINETEEN

Jezabelle stopped in to the Catniption Barkley Clinic to talk to Dr. Dogwood about her recently acquired pets. She needed to make an appointment to check them over.

"I know one of those pets," Dr. Dogwood announced after Jezabelle described her dilemma and described the cat's features to him. "The one you describe that looks like the other cat is named Mrs. Mysterious. She belonged to Fred Rally the baker."

"You knew Fred?"

"Only because of his cat—quiet fellow, not much to say, good-looking young man and a very talented baker. Kept to himself. Don't even know where he lived; he paid in cash and didn't leave an address. I was sorry to hear about his death."

"What about Mr. Shifty? He was always trying to sneak into Annabelle's house."

Dr. Dogwood shook his head. "Have no idea about that one. I do know Fred said that there was a cat always trying to sneak in to visit Mrs. Mysterious. He didn't know where it came from."

"Are you sure you don't know where Fred lived?" Jezabelle asked again.

"Nope. Said he had a beautiful house in a nice neighborhood. Lots of history, he said. That's all I can tell you. Bring your Mr. Shifty in and I'll check him out. I don't need to see Mrs. Mysterious. She was just here a few weeks ago."

"If you think of anything else that you can remember about where Fred lived, call me," Jezzy said as she opened the door to leave.

"I've already told the police all I know."

"The police know about this?" Jezabelle would have to talk to Hank for not giving her all these details. It might have something to do with the break-ins in her neighborhood. Maybe she'd have to offer him some whipped cream herself. Jezabelle left the vet clinic.

"Hey, Jezabelle! Come on over and have some coffee!" Jiffy Jacks was motioning to Jezabelle from in front of the Brilliant Bistro. "It's lunchtime. I'll fix you my special Lalopalo Sandwich."

Jezabelle waved back. "Sorry, Jiff, I'm on my way to an interview."

"Oh, is Snoop Steckle interviewing you about the break-ins in your neighborhood? I saw him earlier here with Hank Hardy. Hank looked none too pleased by their conversation."

"Gotta go!" Jezabelle gave a final wave, getting in her car and driving to her street. She parked her car in her garage and walked across the street to Miranda Covington's house. She didn't imagine Miranda would answer, but she rang the doorbell anyway.

It took twenty-five pushes on the old-fashioned ringer to get Miranda to answer its chimes.

"What?" Miranda shouted when she opened the door. Seeing Jezabelle, she apologized, "I'm sorry, Jezabelle, I thought you were that Snoop Steckle. He's been trying to get a story for the *Brilliant Times Chronicle*. I told him I don't know anything but he's relentless. Even tried throwing stones at my office window to get me to come to the door. Come on in."

Jezabelle looked around the entryway and into the living room. "Beautiful house. It has a little different layout than mine."

"I love it. It's the perfect house for a mystery writer. I keep finding new hidden spaces that I didn't know were here. What can I do for you?"

Jezabelle leaned in close. "Can I trust you?"

Miranda stepped back to study Jezabelle. "Why?"

"We want you to join our new group, The Penderghast Puzzle Protectors, but you can't tell anyone what we're about. We're undercover."

Miranda slowly nodded her head. "Ah, maybe you should sit down. Can I call anyone for you?"

"I'm serious."

"I'm sure you are. Perhaps all the excitement has been too much for you the past few days," Miranda suggested, taking Jezabelle's hand.

Jezabelle frowned. "No, ask the others. We're going to figure out what's happening in our neighborhood, but we need all the neighbors in on this because they each have a piece of the puzzle."

"And this is a secret?"

"Well, I've known HH for a long time and the police department doesn't really approve of citizens getting involved in their investigations, but the way I see it, we have a small police department and right now we have *big* crime and they need all the help we can get."

Miranda nodded her head skeptically. "Ah, I see."

"And what better person to have on our team than a mystery writer. You live with mystery. And you make those mysterious jaunts in the middle of the night." Jezabelle threw that in for good measure thinking she might learn something about Miranda's night-time activities.

Miranda pulled her hand back from Jezabelle's. "I thought I explained that. Baking, remember?"

Jezabelle decided she should agree with Miranda rather than tell her she knew for a fact her baking gig at the Bistro had been over for a little while. "Oh, I'm sorry. I'm a little forgetful at my age. So will you join us?"

Miranda laughed and shook her head as if contemplating the question. "Well, only if I get first rights to write it into a mystery. My lips are sealed until I sign a publishing deal."

Jezabelle stood up. "Great, now we need to talk to Rock Stone after he comes home tonight and we'll be ready for our next move. Oh, and don't let your floor get stolen before then."

CHAPTER TWENTY

Jezabelle decided to bake as she kept an eye out the window, waiting for Rock Stone to come home from his shift at—she frowned—he never did say where he worked. It was strange after living next door to her for the past five years, she'd never asked him where he worked. She saw his car pull into his driveway and up to his garage. He never put his car in the garage at night. Maybe it was because he couldn't wait to have his cigarette. She wiped her hands on her apron and left her house through the back door.

"Rock! Don't you know smoking is bad for you, especially at ten o'clock at night?"

Rock jumped, not having seen Jezabelle coming near him in the dark.

"Jezabelle... you... scared... me. Thought... it... might... be the... floornappers."

"They napped already today at my house, that's why I wanted to talk to you. We checked out your floor today," Jezabelle informed him.

"We? Who... is... we? I... said... *you* not... a... *we.*"

"We've formed a neighborhood group but it's secret and we want you to join."

Rock thought before answering. "Do... the... police... know about... this... group?"

"No and you can't tell them or anyone but those in the neighborhood," Jezabelle warned.

A grin came across his face, "Then... I'm in. What... do we... do first?"

"We tear up the squares in your floor and Phoebe's floor and see what's underneath. Maybe that's what the floornappers are looking for," Jezabelle suggested.

"Why... would... they... take the... pieces... of the... floor... if... they wanted... what... was... underneath it?"

Jezabelle wrinkled up her nose. "Good point. I didn't think you had it in you, Rock." Jezabelle nodded her head. "Glad you're in. You might actually help us. Welcome to the Penderghast Puzzle Protectors. I'll be in touch—I have to finish my baking."

Rock smiled. It threw Jezabelle off for a minute because she wasn't used to him smiling. "Or... are... you... waiting... for your... visitor?" Before Jezabelle could answer, he ground out his cigarette and walked toward his house.

Jezabelle hurried back to her house thinking she needed to keep an eye on Rock; he was sharper than she suspected. Her nose picked up the scent that told her the cheesecake she'd put in the oven was almost done. She still had cupcakes and muffins to bake. She did her best thinking while she was baking. The sugar from her delectable goodies seemed to make her brain sharper.

Once she had her baking under control again, she picked up her cell phone. When she heard the voice answer on the other end of the line, she cautioned, "Someone's on to us. We have to be careful. Remember, I told you, no one can know about us or it's over. I don't need everyone talking about our relationship until we know what it is."

"Jezabelle, my sweetie, what do you want me to do?" The voice on the other end of the line became anxious.

"Instead of you coming here, I'll meet you at the old barn on the edge of Rooster Pond. The Darnel family still owns the farm but no one lives there anymore. The house is still there along with the barn. No one will see us there. Do you know where it is?"

The voice on the other end of the phone laughed. "I do. It's been a few years. Perfect spot, sweetie, and good idea. See you at 1:00 a.m. on the dot."

Jezabelle heard the phone go dead. She'd better hurry. It was a few minutes after eleven, and she still had to finish her baking and change for her rendezvous at the barn.

CHAPTER TWENTY-ONE

Jezabelle's eyes were foggy the next morning. She didn't get home until almost 3:00 a.m. It had been a beautiful spring evening, and she'd stayed at the barn and the pond longer than she'd expected. The light of the moon over the pond seemed to keep her from leaving.

She heard the garbage truck down the street. Looking at the clock, she realized how late it was and that she hadn't yet put her garbage out. Pulling on her Mickey Mouse robe and fluffy slippers, she trotted down the steps and out the back door, grabbing her garbage can and pulling it down the driveway. She made it to the end of her driveway just as Hickory pulled up with the garbage truck.

"Hi, Hick!" Jezabelle smiled and winked at the garbage man.

"Hey, Jezabelle!" Hickory winked back. "Did you wear that Mickey Mouse robe just for me?" Hick twitched his eyebrows making them pop up and down on purpose.

Laughing, Jezabelle answered, "Of course, I did; you're such a youngster that I thought old Mickey might make you want to play."

"Jezabelle, what would my mother say, you flirting with me?" Hickory laughed.

"Have you seen your mother flirt with the meter man?" Jezabelle innocently asked. "We're harmless, just giving you some practice so when you meet the barracudas of the world you're safe."

Phoebe stuck her head out her door as she let Jasper out of the house. "Woo hoo, Jezabelle! Hi, Hick!"

Jezabelle nodded in Phoebe's direction. "Speaking of barracudas, I better see what she wants. Enjoy the rest of your day, Hick."

Hick dumped the garbage into the truck. "Almost done here. I have to go and dig a grave on a private cemetery."

"Dig a grave?" Phoebe asked overhearing the conversation.

"I moonlight once in a while. I help the Brilliant Grave Diggers' Association occasionally. They're getting up in age so I said I'd help them. They still dig graves by hand you know. Something about the forefathers having the stipulation that all graves are sacred and the ground shouldn't be touched by machines. Although I don't know why Brilliant hasn't changed those rules because there weren't machines to dig graves as far as I know back in the dark ages when the Brilliant Brothers lived?"

"Diggity Dig," Phoebe sang.

"Diggity Dog," Jezabelle sang back.

Both Phoebe and Jezabelle broke into loud laughter.

"Now I know it's time to go. Have a nice day, ladies!" Hick hopped onto the seat in his garbage truck and drove away.

"Nice boy," Jezabelle commented.

"So what's the plan?" Phoebe asked.

"I talked to Miranda and Rock. They're in. I'll call Lizzy, Miranda, and Rock, and you call Warbler. We have to meet after Rock gets home, otherwise he'll miss the fun. Tell them we'll meet at Rock's tomorrow night at ten thirty. We'll start with his floor."

"Does Miranda know we're going to tear up her floor too?" Phoebe threw out the question knowing that at times Jezabelle tended to leave some details out when she was talking someone into something.

"I might have forgotten to mention it. But her house is designed completely differently than ours. And... she doesn't seem too worried about the floornappers."

Phoebe shrugged her shoulders and answered with disdain in her voice, "Of course not, Jezabelle, she's used to dealing with murder and all kinds of dastardly things in her books. Maybe she's encountered them in real life so nothing scares her."

"Well, I guess we'll find out. I guess I'd better exchange Mickey for some street duds. We'll see you tomorrow night." Jezabelle walked away and into her house before Phoebe could come up with some other hare-brained idea for the day.

Jezabelle's cell phone was ringing when she got in her door. The name on the phone flashed *Phoebe*. Apparently, Phoebe wouldn't let it go and had something more to say. "Yup," Jezabelle answered looking out the window at Phoebe standing in the middle of the road talking on the cell phone.

"Who's going to take the first shift today? We forgot to designate," Phoebe asked.

"First shift for what?"

"To watch for the floornappers. They might come back if they think none of us are home. Do you have a shotgun I can borrow?"

Jezabelle plastered her face to the window and glared at Phoebe. "I am not giving you a shotgun. You might be younger than me, but your aim is terrible. Remember the arcade the last time the carnival was in town? You missed the ducks and hit the mayor's hat, knocking it off his head. I think you got charged with reckless duck mischief. But you might be right about tricking the floornappers into thinking no one's home."

"There are only three houses left that haven't been touched: mine, Miranda's, and Rock's, and we don't want the floors to disappear before we tear them up, do we? In case something is hidden underneath?" Phoebe's voice was getting more excited and more garbled the faster she talked.

"Phoebe, you're home, Miranda's home. Just watch your own houses. I'll watch Rock's. And stay out of sight!" Jezabelle ordered. "I'll talk to you tomorrow. Jezabelle hung up the phone, walked through her house and peeked out the back window. Everything was quiet except for Jasper and Max digging in the weeds by her garage. She wasn't going to disturb them. They were the best weed pullers in Brilliant.

CHAPTER TWENTY-TWO

Jezabelle, Phoebe, Lizzy, Miranda, and Mr. Warbler were waiting by Rock Stone's back door when he drove into his driveway and up to his garage. He always parked to the right of his garage door. He revved the engine twice, got out of his car, and lit up a cigarette all the while keeping an eye on his waiting visitors.

"He could hurry up before anyone sees us," Phoebe complained.

"Well, a man has to do what he has to do when he gets home from a hard day at work," Mr. Warbler defended Rock's behavior.

Jezabelle made a muffled sound before saying, "Or he could be delaying meeting with us. Maybe he has something to hide. Hey, Rock! Why don't you ever park in your garage?"

Rock Stone ground out his cigarette and slowly walked over to the group. "I... have... a lot... of valuables... stored... in... there that... won't... fit in... my... house. It's... only a... one-car... garage."

"Did the police examine your piece of floor?" Miranda asked.

"Yes, but... they... didn't... try to... remove... it. Just... took down... what... was carved... on... it."

"Why are we taking it up? I forgot to ask, but I brought my chainsaw." Mr. Warbler held up the chainsaw that had been laying by his feet.

Lizzy, quiet up until now, swatted Mr. Warbler in the arm. "Because we're missing something. Maybe they weren't entirely after the floor but what was underneath it."

Miranda held up a crowbar. "I brought a crowbar just in case."

Rock Stone made a face that reminded Jezabelle of a bad kiss on a Sunday morning.

"You... own... a... crowbar?"

"Yes, Rock, I do own a crowbar and I'm ready to destroy your floor," Miranda answered with a clang of the crowbar on the metal railing by the steps.

"Okay, we better get crackin' before it's morning. Open the door, Rock," Jezabelle ordered.

Rock opened the door, turned on the lights, and led the group up the stairs to the bedroom with the carved floor.

"Have you ever torn up a floor before, Jezabelle?" Lizzy asked while surveying the square piece of floor that was large enough to fall through if they made a mistake.

"No, but how hard can it be? Warbler make the cut, but be careful, we don't want to go through the ceiling downstairs. If this is like the others, there's a pocket underneath framed in a square."

"Phoebe, you be the lookout." Lizzy led Phoebe over to the window. "If you see anyone coming here, warn us."

"They'll be able to see me from the window," Phoebe protested.

"Cut the lights!" Jezabelle ordered.

"You... can't... cut... the... lights. Warbler... will kill... us... all... with that... chainsaw... not to... mention... my floor."

"Yah, haven't you ever heard of the chainsaw massacre? What was that state anyway?" Phoebe shivered as she recalled the movie.

"Stone, you got any flashlights?" Jezabelle queried.

"No. I... always... use... the... flashlight... on my... cellphone."

"Great idea. Cut the lights and turn on your cell phone flashlights so Warbler can see and let's get started." Jezabelle walked over and flipped the light switch at the same time turning on her cellphone flashlight. The others followed her lead.

Mr. Warbler started his chainsaw and began to make a cut. "Isn't there a better saw to use rather than a chainsaw?" Lizzy suggested. "Aren't chainsaws for trees?"

Mr. Warbler cut the power on the saw. "This is the only saw I have. I use it to take care of my yard and my trees. Besides, I noticed this piece of floor is thicker than the rest. Let me work—I know what I'm doing." He revved up the chainsaw again.

"Be careful; we don't want to go all the way through," Jezabelle warned.

Warbler made a cut around the edges of the piece of floor. He chipped just enough so the floor came loose in the square.

"Stop!" Miranda ordered. "I've got this." She moved her crowbar in place and lifted one side of the floor.

The others moved forward, putting down their flashlights and grabbing the side of the tile while Miranda worked her way around the square. Phoebe moved from the window to hold the flashlight so they could see. They lifted the square away from the hole and all turned their lights back to the hole in the floor. A lone piece of old paper was the only thing occupying the empty square.

Rock Stone leaned down, picked it up, and shone his light on the paper. "It's... a bible... verse."

They all crowded around Rock. Jezabelle took the piece of paper from him. "I'll read it," Jezabelle volunteered, knowing she'd be impatient waiting for Rock's slow drawl to spit out the verse. "It says, *And now abideth faith, hope, charity, these three; but the greatest of these is charity*."

Phoebe wrinkled her nose in thought. "That's from the Bible, but I haven't heard it that way. Shouldn't the last word have been *love*?"

"No, the modern version is *love* but this is from the King James Version. I recognize it because I used a verse from King James in one of my books recently," Miranda explained.

"Do you suppose my floor had a bible verse under it? What does it mean or is it just a fluke?" Mr. Warbler prattled on.

"Well, it must have something to do with what's carved into this piece of the floor," Jezabelle concluded.

"But why steal a piece of the floor to get to a piece of paper?" Lizzy asked.

"Put... the... floor... back down. It... will... sit on... the... frame... of the floor... so I... don't... forget... and fall... through... the hole," Rock instructed.

"We need to put the pieces together. It's late, way past my bedtime," Jezabelle told the group. "Let's think about this and meet up tomorrow at the library in the Brilliant Brothers' Room and work on our puzzle."

"Good idea; I need to stop by the library to pick up the names for the contest," Phoebe informed the group. "You can help me pick out the name."

Rock Stone shook his head. "You... will... have... to fill... me in. I... have to... work."

"I'll keep the bible verse." Jezabelle put the paper in her pocket.

"Jezabelle, do you want to go to the Brilliant Bistro for lunch after the meeting?" Lizzy asked.

"Why don't we all go?" Miranda invited herself. "I don't get out during the day—ever. I'm so busy writing. It might be fun and then you can all come back to my house, and I can show you some of the hidden nooks I've found in my house."

"Or, we could go to my house and lift up my floor and see what's under it. Maybe I'll do that tonight," said Phoebe. "Warbler, do you want to bring your chainsaw and come over for a little sawing?" She sidled up next to the large man.

Warbler began to sweat. He moved quickly away from Phoebe. "I, ah, have to make a phone call. I think we should all do it together. Why don't we do that after we have lunch at the Bistro?"

"Be... careful... going... down the... steps," Rock warned. "We... don't... want any... accidents." He grinned but the others couldn't see it in the dark.

Once downstairs and outside, Jezabelle warned the group before they went their separate ways, "Be careful, and watch your floors."

CHAPTER TWENTY-THREE

When Jezabelle arrived at the Brilliant Library the next morning and walked through the Hole in the Wall to the Brilliant Brothers' Room, she found Marion's son, Junior Markowsky, sitting at the puzzle table working on their puzzle. "Junior, I didn't expect to see you here."

"I was visiting Mom before I went to work. My shift starts at noon at Intelligent Icicles and I saw the puzzle. Thought I'd sit down and see what I could do," Junior explained.

Jezabelle looked at the wall. "I see they removed the door and finished the Hole in the Wall entrance to the room. It looks great. Now all we need is a hole in the wall gang."

"Hi, Jezabelle! Is your group meeting today? I hope you don't mind Junior messing with your puzzle," Marion asked, coming into the room. "Being head librarian is sometimes a hard job. You can't believe all the hoo hah I've heard the past few days about the hole in the wall and the theft of the plat map. And do we have a lot of names for the contest for Phoebe and the committee to choose from!"

"Did I hear my name?" Phoebe entered the room followed by Mr. Warbler and Lizzy.

"You did. Apparently we're going to be busy choosing a name today." Jezabelle winked at the group letting them know they had a slight problem.

Phoebe frowned. "Junior, I didn't see you there. What are you doing?"

"I thought I'd work on this puzzle until I went to work. Mom said you formed a group. What did you say that name was, Mom?" Junior looked at his mother.

"It's called the Penderghast Puzzle Protectors," Lizzy answered. "But right now we're going to work on choosing a name for the library. You can stay if you want but it's probably going to be a long discussion. I heard there were a lot of names."

Confusion showed on Mr. Warbler's face. "But... I... thought we were going to... "

"Go out to lunch." Jezabelle grabbed his arm and led him over to a chair while giving him a glaring look. "But that's later."

Miranda rushed into the room. "You'll never guess what I..." She stopped mid-sentence when she realized Marion and Junior were in the room.

"Well, Miranda Covington! I wasn't sure you still lived here. A famous author like you. I've been trying to get a hold of you to do a book signing at the library, but you haven't answered your phone. I thought I had your old phone number or you had moved out of town," Marion rambled on.

"Ah, just visiting. My dear Jezabelle talked me into meeting here today." She walked over and gave Jezabelle a hug.

Jezabelle put both hands on Miranda's arms and moved her back, stepping around Miranda and over to Marion. "Yes, we thought a famous author should help us choose the name."

Marion caught Junior's eye. "Junior, it's important we get this name change done. Perhaps you should leave this group alone. You can work on the puzzle another time."

"Well, Mom, if you think I should leave, I will."
Junior stood up from the table. "It's been fun. I'll
see you soon. Let me know when you have a
meeting of the Penderghast Puzzle Protectors.
Perhaps I'll join."

The group stood silent as Junior left the Brilliant
Brothers' Room.

"I'll leave you to it," Marion said, as she exited
the room behind Junior.

"Now what?" Lizzy asked.

"We go through the names while we talk about
our puzzle. But keep it down so no one hears,"
Jezabelle warned.

They all sat down at the table as Marion
suddenly walked back into the room and presented
them with a notebook of all the names that had been
entered in the contest.

"Good luck! This is quite a bunch." Marion
shook her head as she left muttering, "I'm glad I
don't have to do the choosing."

"We have our work cut out for us," Phoebe said,
glancing at the list.

"But first, I have to tell you what I found out
about the Brilliant Brothers," Miranda interjected.
"They were secret puzzle masters. All of the boys
had a passion for creating puzzles in real life, but
they did it under another name—Roosevelt Strong."

"That's our street name and the name of the
street that it intersects with on the corner," Phoebe
noted.

"How did you find all this out?" Lizzy asked.

"I've been doing research online for some time. I
wondered about my house having all these little
hidden nooks. Last night when I went home, I
snooped around to see if I could find a new nook.
It's been a game of mine since I moved into the

house. I've found some pretty interesting stuff. Anyway, last night I found an old puzzle book by Roosevelt Strong. So I did an Internet search for the name and found the company that published their books. I couldn't believe it's been in business since the late 1800s. They only publish unique books now, but they kept their history quite well. The person I talked to looked up Roosevelt Strong and the company's records on that author. It appears they put out many puzzle books under that name, but it was in the contract that the author's real names never be known. The woman I spoke to says there are no living relatives and the books no longer are for sale, so she thought it would be fine to give me the information. The Brilliant Brothers are Roosevelt Strong!"

A loud crash sounded near the door. The group saw books falling on the floor that had been stacked on a ladder by the door waiting to be put on the shelves outside the room.

Jezabelle picked up the notebook with the names. "I suggest we name the library the Lackadaisical Meandering," she said loudly so anyone listening outside the room could hear.

Lizzy jumped up excitedly. "Oh, that's my name. I won! I won!"

Jezabelle pulled her best friend down in the chair and whispered, "Lizzy, I know that's your name. I just said that in case whoever knocked the books off that ladder was listening."

"I like that name!" Phoebe declared. "And since Lizzy is a member of the committee, I will donate the $5,000.00 to the Brilliant Christmas Fund to give out free books at Christmas time. It's all settled. All in favor say *aye!*"

A general mumbling of *aye*s could be heard.

"Meeting adjourned!" declared Phoebe.

Mr. Warbler picked up a puzzle piece. "Let's work on this puzzle. I've got part of a butterfly!"

CHAPTER TWENTY-FOUR

Red Hannahan, Jet Pilager, George Grifter, and Cal Phillips were sitting around one of the tables in the Brilliant Bistro when the Penderghast Puzzle Protectors came in for lunch.

"Hey, Warbler, glad to see you, hope you're no worse for wear from your fall," Jet Pillager commented as they walked past their table.

Red Hannahan stood up and offered his chair to Miranda. "I don't believe we've met. I'm Red Hannahan. Won't you join us? And you are—" He held out his hand to Miranda.

"Miranda Covington, and thank you but I think Jiffy has a table saved for us in the corner."

Lizzy giggled and said to Red, "I'll make sure she calls you if she has a fire she needs putting out. In fact, we could arrange that." She winked at Red and proceeded to join the others at the table.

"What can I get you?" Jiffy asked the group. "I have an excellent Poof Omelet filled with Brussel sprouts, tomatoes, cheese, and mushrooms for the special."

The group quickly buried their heads in the menu.

"I think I'll have the Jiffy Burger," Jezabelle decided. The others all nodded their heads, agreeing and ordering the same thing.

"Look, isn't that Rock Stone talking to Hank Hardy in the alley?" Phoebe nudged Jezabelle, as she pointed out the window.

Jezabelle peered through the window. "It looks like it, but he has his back turned to us and he's too far away."

The others leaned across the table to look out the window. Mr. Warbler frowned, "It's quite a distance away. I don't have my glasses."

"They're leaving now but I think that was Rock," Phoebe insisted.

"But he said he had to work," Lizzy reminded them.

"Does anyone know where he works?" Warbler asked.

They all shrugged their shoulders.

"Say, Warbler, you're among friends, and Miranda, you're here too. What were you two up to in Annabelle's yard a few days ago?" Phoebe asked.

"Yes and I saw you coming back from there the other night again, Warbler," Jezabelle added.

"You went back over there?" Miranda eagle-eyed Warbler.

"Well, uh…" Warbler tried to come up with an answer but was interrupted when Jiffy Jacks brought their food.

He unloaded his tray and put the burgers in front of each of them. He took a piece of chocolate cream pie and set it in front of Jezabelle.

Jezabelle frowned. "I didn't order any pie."

Jiffy smiled and said, "No, sweetie, but *someone* did and they said to tell you *sweets for the sweet.*"

Jezabelle blushed while the others stared at Jezabelle to see her reaction.

"First flowers, now sweets. Are you keeping something from your old friend, Jezzy?" HH leaned over Jezabelle's shoulder.

Jezabelle ignored his taunt. "Are you keeping anything from *us*? Have you found out anything about the floornapper?"

"I was about to ask this group that very question." Hank directed a stern look at the group. "I hear we now have a new group in town called the Penderghast Puzzle Protectors. Would you mind explaining?"

"We meet at the library and we put puzzles together. Ask Marion and Junior; they'll tell you. We've met twice," Jezabelle informed him.

"And who told you?" Phoebe asked, thinking of the possibility of HH talking to Rock Stone in the alley.

"Actually, Snoop Steckle told me. Apparently Marion is putting an article in the paper about the new name chosen for the library and also details about your new group."

Shock covered the faces of the Penderghast Puzzle Protectors. "She did what?" They all spoke simultaneously.

"She did! But I suspect there's more to this group than meets the eye. Speaking of eyes, I'll be keeping my eye on you. And Jezzy, don't let the sweet nothings you're receiving turn your head. There also might be more than meets the eye there." Hank turned, nodded to the fireman at the next table, and left the Bistro.

The group sat in silence until Phoebe said, "I think we should adjourn to my house. Since eyes seem to have been the primary subject here, do I hear any *ayes*?

CHAPTER TWENTY-FIVE

"At least we have a heads up on the article," Jezabelle addressed the group while sipping the tea that Phoebe had made when they all descended upon her house.

"Do you suppose we can get Snoop to stop it?" Lizzy asked. "We don't want every Jack, John, and Jerry trying to join. After all, we're here for the sole purpose of solving the murder and the crime."

"If we do that," Miranda answered, "Snoop will be all over this. He didn't get the nickname of *Snoop* for nothing."

"Well, let's put the pieces together." Mr. Warbler rubbed his hands in anticipation of putting together a puzzle no matter what kind.

Miranda snapped her fingers. "Maybe that's what we need to do. Phoebe, do you have a large sheet of paper?"

Jezabelle nodded her head. "Yes, let's put it on paper and see what we have and then we'll check out Phoebe's floor. Are you sure, Miranda, that you don't have any floor pieces like the ones that have been stolen?"

Miranda shook her head. "My floors are beautiful and in pristine condition. I walked them all and they are plain hardwood floors with no designs. Each corner of the floor in each room has a small wooden block with the letter B in it. But other than that—"

Phoebe handed Miranda a large sheet of paper and a pen.

Miranda asked, "Okay, Jezabelle, your floor had three boxes plus a little cross in the corner." Miranda drew three boxes in the middle of the paper.

"Rock Stone's floor had the words *faith, hope,* and *charity*," Lizzy added.

Miranda put the words underneath the boxes.

Jezabelle thought for a minute. "Put the names on the boxes."

Miranda erased the names from underneath the boxes and put them on the boxes.

They all looked at the drawing. "Now what?" Phoebe asked. "We don't know what was on Warbler's except for the cross, or on Annabelle's."

"We look at the square in your floor. Where is it?" Miranda asked.

"It's in the sunroom." Phoebe got up and motioned the others to follow.

"What is that?" Warbler asked, gazing at the piece of floor.

"It's just leaves around the edge. Stacked leaves with branches," Lizzy added.

"And a cross in the corner. Not really a picture," Jezabelle surmised.

"Well, let me get my chainsaw and let's pull it up and see what's underneath." Mr. Warbler rubbed his hands together in gleeful anticipation of getting to use his chainsaw again.

"Get your chainsaw. I have my own crowbar," Phoebe instructed as she ran out of the room to find her crowbar. Mr. Warbler followed but exited through the front door to head for his garage.

Jezabelle paced the sun porch and looked at the floor. "Have you ever noticed the pattern in these

Seedorf 107

hardwood floors? They aren't laid out the way normal hardwood floors are."

Miranda looked down at the floor. "You're right. Mine is the standard layout but this one has a strange pattern."

The rev of a chainsaw interrupted their musings. Warbler was back. Phoebe entered the room with a crowbar at the same time.

"Let's get started!" Warbler's eyes were bright with excitement.

He gently put the chainsaw to the floor and etched out the square, going around it a few times until he had it loose. Phoebe put the crowbar in place and lifted. The others helped get the big piece of floor up.

Jezabelle turned around. "Did something flash?" She looked around the room and out the window.

The others shook their heads. "We didn't see anything," Miranda said.

"Look, another piece of paper!" Warbler pointed to the object.

Lizzy bent down and picked it up. They all crowded around Lizzy.

"What does it say? What does it say?" Phoebe was jumping up and down like a jackrabbit.

"It says, *Hast not thou made a hedge about him, and about his house, and about all that he hath on every side? Thou hast blessed the work of his hands, and his substance is increased in the land,*" Lizzy read the words on the piece of paper.

"What?" Warbler asked.

"It's another bible verse," Jezabelle answered.

Miranda pulled up her cell phone and punched in the words. "It's from Job: 1:10."

"I don't get it. What does a bible verse have to do with any of this?" Lizzy asked.

Miranda was studying the leaves on the floor. "Do you suppose this is a hedge?" And the hedge is serving as protection for something?"

The group studied the carving on the piece of floor.

"The floor is a puzzle piece." Warbler pointed to the cross. "This isn't a cross; it's a plus sign to add the pieces together."

Miranda ran into the living room and picked up her paper and pen. She drew a hedge around the boxes. "So what does that look like?"

"Tombstones," Jezabelle stated. "Tombstones."

"Warbler, you have to remember what was on your piece of floor." Jezabelle grabbed both of Mr. Warbler's arms and gave them a shake.

Lizzy pulled Jezabelle back. "Warby, relax and close your eyes. Think back, you're getting up in the morning. You look down at the floor and gaze at its beauty. What do you see?" Lizzy's tone was soft and soothing.

"Warby, Warby?" Jezabelle cackled breaking the mood.

"Jezabelle, I was trying to get him to remember," Lizzy chastised her best friend.

"I remember! I remember!" Warbler shouted.

"You do?" the group asked in amazement.

Looking sheepish, Warbler hung his head. "Well, I remember I have an old picture of my floor. I took it when I moved into the house because I thought it was so unusual. If I could just remember where it is."

"Well, Warby, you go home and remember. It's getting late and I have to do some baking." Jezabelle pushed him toward the door relishing her new name for their neighbor.

Miranda looked at the time on her cell phone. "You're right. I'm way behind in my writing. Who knew going outside during the day could be so much fun."

"Now we have to figure out what the stolen plat map has to do with these shenanigans," Jezabelle instructed the group. "Think about it tonight and we'll get together tomorrow. And maybe by then Warbler will have found his picture. Thankfully, no one else has been a victim of the floornapper."

"Do you suppose they've already figured out the puzzle?" Phoebe asked.

"And what the treasure is? What they're looking for and who they are?" Lizzy rattled on in her own little world.

"That's for them to know and us to find out," Jezabelle added. "And we will!"

CHAPTER TWENTY–SIX

It was Jezabelle's phone that woke her up the next morning, not her alarm clock.

"So... what... did you... find... out? Did... you... figure... anything... out?" Rock's slow speech told Jezabelle who was on the other end of the line.

"We did, Rock, but I don't want to talk it about it over the phone."

"I... am... on my... way... to work. Can... we... meet... tonight... for an... update?"

"Ten o'clock?" Jezabelle asked.

"I... have... to stop... at... the Brilliant... Bedazzle... Brewery... to talk to... someone. Why... don't... we all... meet there?"

"At the brewery? Well, I don't know. I've never been there, but do they serve wine?"

"You... have... never been... to the... new... brewery?"

"No, but I'll check with the others. Are you sure we should meet in public?"

"I... might... have... a lead... for our... puzzle. But... you... have to... see... it... and it's... at the brewery."

"Later then, Rock. I'll let the others know but I've got to go now. I hear the garbage truck."

Jezabelle threw on her clothes, rushed downstairs and out the back, grabbed her garbage can, and pulled it to the front just as Hick was pulling up.

Hick greeted Jezabelle when he got out of the truck. "Jezabelle, great picture of you on the front page of the *Brilliant Times Chronicle*." Hick's eyes were twinkling with mirth and he was trying hard not to laugh. Jezabelle's confused expression gave him just the push he needed to break out in laughter.

"What are you talking about?"

"You haven't read the paper yet? Seems the Penderghast Puzzle Protectors are a front for floornapping activity."

"What?" Jezabelle screamed.

Hick, still laughing, jumped into his truck. "I've got some graves to dig. I'm sorry our relationship has to be over," he teased. "You might be a bad influence on me." Still laughing, Hickory drove off.

Jezabelle ran to her front porch and picked up the newspaper lying right outside her door. There on the front page was a picture of Mr. Warbler with his chainsaw, Phoebe with her crowbar, and Miranda, Jezabelle, and Lizzy lifting the piece of floor in Phoebe's house! She knew she'd seen a flash! That pesky Snoop Steckle must have been window peeping.

A car pulled up in Jezabelle's driveway. Another car pulled up in Phoebe's driveway. HH and Steve Stick got out of the car in her driveway. Hanna and Jeb got out of the car in Phoebe's driveway. Jezabelle watched as Hanna walked over to Mr. Warbler's house and Jeb continued on to Phoebe's door. Hank came to join Jezabelle while Stick walked down the street and across to Miranda's house.

"HH, what brings you here so early in the morning?" Jezabelle feigned innocence.

Hank Hardy shook his head and pointed to the newspaper. "Ah, I see you've seen the paper.

Would you mind telling me what you were doing? It looks rather suspicious."

"We were helping her level her floor. With all this hoopla with the floors, we were pondering her piece when we noticed it wasn't level so we were trying to fix it." Jezabelle's look challenged HH to disagree.

"Arrest him, not me!" Phoebe's loud voice could be heard across the street as Hanna was leading Phoebe to the police car. "That Snoop Steckle was window peeping. He's the one who should be arrested."

Hanna raised her voice to shout over Phoebe's so Phoebe would hear her through her ranting. "We're not arresting you, we're just going down to the station for questioning."

Jezabelle saw Miranda walking up to them accompanied by Steve Stick.

"I can't believe I'm out of the house during the day two days in a row," Miranda could be overheard talking to Steve. "This is exciting for a mystery writer."

"Stop! I have to feed my squirrels and the birds before you haul me in. I'm responsible for their well-being, you know." Mr. Warbler was on his front lawn and Jeb was allowing Warbler to feed his animals.

Jezabelle looked at Hank. "Is this necessary?"

"Come on, Jezzy, we're just taking you all in to question you. You have to know that you've been caught in a compromising position. Ouch!"

Mr. Shifty and Mrs. Mysterious had at that moment entrapped both of HH's legs in a claw trap and showed no signs of letting him go. "Call them off, Jezzy!"

Jezabelle laughed. She waited for a few seconds, watching Hanna and Jeb drive away with Phoebe and Mr. Warbler. "Ok, HH. Come on, you two. Since you've decided to be my protector cats, I'll put you in the house to guard it." She took the cats off HH's legs but not without a few ouches being muttered from his lips.

Jezabelle glanced back as she and Miranda were led to the waiting car. She thought she saw the shade move in Rock Stone's house but when she looked back for a second time, the shade was in place.

CHAPTER TWENTY-SEVEN

Sadie Noir looked up from her desk and caught Jezabelle's eye. Jezabelle rolled her eyes at Sadie and commented, "Hi, Sadie; it looks like we'll be sharing your office for a short time."

Sadie was the desk person for the Brilliant Police Department and kept track of all the comings and goings. "Sorry about this, Jezabelle. I tried to talk HH out of bringing all of you in. I know you didn't do anything."

"Well, at least one person in this office has some common sense." Phoebe directed a haughty glance at Hank Hardy. "You arrest that Snoop Steckle for window peeping! I want to file charges!"

Hank looked at the group and said to his deputies, "Make them comfortable in the break room." He turned to the group. "We'll talk to you soon. We want to go over your stories among ourselves to see how they match up."

"Do we need a lawyer, Hank?" Miranda was thumbing through her cell phone contacts.

Hanna Hardy stepped forward. "No, we just need to question you about what you were doing at Phoebe's house and see if it matches the other crimes that have been committed."

"You're not under arrest but... if you don't cooperate you might be," Steve Stick warned the group.

"We have nothing to hide." Jezabelle pulled herself up to her full five feet.

Warbler looked at Jezabelle. "We don't?"

Jezabelle skewered Warbler with a warning look.

"I mean, we don't!" Warbler stated emphatically.

Sadie got up from her desk and gestured toward the back room. "Why don't you all come in here? I'll get you some coffee while you're waiting and you can even turn the television on, right, Hank?"

"Fine, we'll be in shortly." Hank nodded toward the back room.

Once in the room with the door shut, Lizzy turned toward the group. "What did you tell them?"

"Shh!" Jezabelle pointed to the ceiling. "Someone's probably listening."

Miranda walked over, turned the television louder, and motioned the group to come over by the television. "This will drown out our whispers."

"It sure will; we won't even be able to hear us." Jezabelle's sarcastic tone was lost in the noise of the television.

"I told them I was remodeling my floor, and I wanted the piece to be turned around the other way," Phoebe told the group.

"I said we were going to build a fire pit in the middle of the room for warmth in the wintertime," Mr. Warbler chimed in.

The group turned to look at him. "What? Did I say something wrong?" Warbler asked.

"Did you ever think a fire pit in the middle of a wood floor in the house might raise suspicion when the fireplace is steps away and a fire pit could cause a fire?" Jezabelle swatted him playfully on his shoulder.

"I told them we were practicing a scene in my latest mystery to see if it would work," Miranda added.

The door opened and Lizzy walked into the room. The door was shut firmly behind her.

"Lizzy, I see they decided you should join us too," Miranda welcomed Lizzy.

"I told them the truth," Lizzy stated.

"And that would be?" Jezabelle and the others waited for the answer.

"That we wanted to see what it looked like under the floor before someone stole it. We saw the *after* but we've never seen the *before*." Lizzy giggled, remembering the look on Jeb Jardene's face when she began to cry loudly after telling him the tale. He was so flummoxed over her tears he quit questioning her and tried to comfort her.

"Well, that's just great. We should have gotten our stories straight before this," Jezabelle chided the group.

"What did you tell Hank?" Miranda asked.

"Never mind; it didn't live up to the imaginativeness of your stories." Jezabelle plopped herself down in a chair. "I guess we wait."

Sadie entered the room with coffee and cinnamon rolls. "I ran over to the Brilliant Bistro and picked up some morning treats for you. Hank and the rest were called out on an emergency and they said to keep you here. Jiffy said he'd send over lunch."

"Lunch—we won't be out of here by lunch?" Miranda paced the floor. I'm behind in my writing."

"They can't keep us here," Phoebe pointed out.

Sadie warned, "No but they'd just come and get you again. Apparently your stories didn't match, and if you leave, they'll just get Judge Jeffries to issue an arrest warrant."

"On what charges?" Mr. Warbler challenged.

Sadie turned to leave. "I can't say; I just work here but I'd recommend you all stay. Here are some cards. Play a game." Sadie took a deck of cards out of her pocket and threw them on the table.

The group sat down at the large table in the room. Jezabelle poured coffee while Lizzy passed out the cinnamon rolls. Miranda shuffled the cards.

"Anyone got something to write the score on? What are we playing?" Phoebe asked.

Mr. Warbler reached in his pocket and pulled out a white piece of paper. "We can write on this."

Jezabelle stared at the paper for a minute. "What's on the other side? It looks like a picture." Reaching for the paper, she turned it over.

"Warbler," Jezabelle addressed the man, "when were you going to tell us you found the picture of the floor?"

The others stared at the picture lying on the table.

"Ah, this morning, but I forgot I had it. Stuck it in my pocket when Jeb hauled me off down here," Mr. Warbler whispered and pointed to the television.

"It's a tree that's carved into the floor. A beautiful oak tree by the looks of it," Miranda concluded. "I wish I had my drawing. As an artist, as well as being an author, I'd put the tree right behind what we think are tombstones."

Jezabelle picked up the picture and put it in her pocket. She motioned everyone to lean in so they could hear. "We'll investigate this further when we get out of here. We are to meet Rock Stone ten o'clock tonight at the Brewery. He said he has more news."

Mr. Warbler got up, opened the door, and peeked out. Seeing Sadie at her desk he asked, "You don't by any chance have a puzzle here for us to put together? We *are* the Penderghast Puzzle Protectors, after all, and cards just aren't our thing."

CHAPTER TWENTY-EIGHT

The day passed slowly at the police station. Jezabelle opened the door and yelled out to Sadie, "It's four o'clock! We've been in here all day. We've put together all the puzzles that you gave us! Where are Hank and his crew?"

"Just talked to him. He said to sit tight and don't leave or he will issue a warrant for your arrest!" Sadie warned, poking her head inside the door. "Why don't you watch a movie? We have a movie channel here that we let the prisoners watch. I was just coming in. Here. Jiffy just dropped off this cheesecake and said he'd be back later with your dinner if you weren't sprung yet."

Jezabelle grabbed the cheesecake and slammed the door on Sadie so loud that the windows rattled. "I think we should break out of this joint. There is *nice* and then there is *nice*, and I'm not either of them right now."

Lizzy giggled and walked over to Jezabelle. "Do you remember when we thought your brother stole our prom dresses? We had a long wait under the bed then too."

"Your brother stole your prom dresses?" Miranda asked.

Lizzy nodded her head. "Yes, he did, but we needed to catch him. So we searched his room and crawled under the bed waiting for him to come back with his friends. We thought maybe we'd hear him telling his friends what he had done."

Jezabelle laughed. "Yes, we were stuck in the room half the night. He decided to invite one of his friends over and they never left the room all night!"

"We lay under that bed all night until finally we could hear they were both asleep somewhere around five in the morning," Lizzy explained.

"Didn't your mother miss you?" Phoebe asked.

"No, she was gone and my dad thought I went with her and back then there were no cell phones so he couldn't call." Jezabelle eyes twinkled as she remembered.

"So, did you get out without being caught?" Miranda wondered.

"We did," Lizzy answered.

"What happened to your prom dresses? Did you ever find out?" Mr. Warbler joined the conversation.

Both Jezabelle and Lizzy nodded. "Yup," Jezabelle said, "My brother had taken our dresses, and he and his friend wore them for a skit during a program at prom. There he was up on stage with our dresses on!"

"Lizzy's eyes brightened. "And we made sure he'd never do that again! But that's a story for another day."

Sadie opened the door cautiously and brought in more coffee. She walked over to the television and used her remote to start a movie. "This is the one we have for today." *The Birdman of Alcatraz* began to play on the television.

"You don't have any more recent movies?" Jezabelle cringed at the picture on the screen.

"Nope, we choose the titles carefully. We want them to be *educational* for our prisoners." Sadie smiled and walked out the door.

The group groaned in unison.

"Maybe we should use this time to get our stories straight," Phoebe suggested.

"A little late for that," Miranda chided.

"Well, I hope we're out in time to meet Rock Stone at the brewery. I've never been there," Lizzy stated.

"I must say my life is certainly busier since I've become involved with my neighbors," Miranda informed the group. "Is this what it's always like during the day?"

"Let's watch the movie; maybe we'll learn something." Mr. Warbler pointed to the screen. "I'm always happy to learn something about birds." He settled back in his chair, eyes glued to the screen.

The others shook their heads and turned their faces to the television. They were deep into the movie when the door to the room opened. Smiling, expecting to see Hank Hardy, their faces fell when they saw Jiffy Jacks pushing a cart.

"Here you are folks! The finest cuisine! Roast chicken, stuffing, mashed potatoes and gravy along with a side of baked beans."

Sadie followed him in. "Hank asked me to stick around until he got back. We can all eat together."

"I think I'm going to call my lawyer." Miranda pulled out her phone. "We've been extremely patient, but I don't see a guard out there and Hank can find us at home."

"No! No!" Jiffy proclaimed. "Stay at least for dinner. I prepared all of this for you. I even baked fresh bread." He pulled a loaf of bread off the bottom of the cart. "And I didn't even have to call the fire department. I'm getting this baking thing down. Pretty soon I'll be as good as this sweetie here." He pointed to Jezabelle.

"Well, the day's wasted anyway." Mr. Warbler, seeing and smelling the food, instantly sat down. "What are a few more hours?"

"Fine," Jezabelle agreed, "but if we aren't out of here by nine-thirty I won't be responsible for my actions. Who did you say your lawyer was, Miranda?"

Miranda put her cell phone away. "I'm so behind in writing my novel." She sat down and grabbed a plate.

"No pickles or carrots?" Phoebe asked as she looked over the food.

The conversation turned to the renaming of the library.

"Does anyone know why the Brilliant brothers named everything after themselves and why no one has renamed anything?" Miranda fished for information.

"I think in the beginning the only people who lived in town were members of the Brilliant brothers' extended family—cousins, etcetera, and the families of those people the brothers had married," Sadie offered what she'd heard. "So it would make sense to name everything after them. It titles them and the town. They owned everything."

"Where did they come from?" Jezabelle asked.

"All I know is that Annabelle Avary was a direct descendant somehow. I seem to remember hearing something about that when she died," Sadie explained further.

The door opened suddenly and Hank Hardy, Hanna, Jeb, and Stick entered the room along with Snoop Steckle.

"There he is! He's the one who caused all this trouble! Arrest him for window peeping!" Jezabelle pointed to Snoop.

"When are you going to let us out of here?" Phoebe screeched.

"And what have you been doing all day long that we had to stay here?" asked Mr. Warbler.

Snoop answered before Hank could. "House fire, arson, suspect driving away. Manhunt close to Fuchsia with the Fuchsia Police force helping and *I* got the scoop!" He held up his camera.

"Yup, all of that *and* I kept you here to keep you safe and out of the way," said Hank. "Somehow I figured you might think this group should be involved in all that too." He scowled at the group intently, then added, "Jiffy, Sadie, Snoop, you three can go now. We have to question these people." Hanna began to clean up the plates to help Jiffy so he could leave.

"I don't mind," said Jiffy. "I'll just clean up here. Go ahead with your conversation." He waited for them to resume talking.

"I think not." Hank waited until Hanna had shuffled them out the door. "Now, do you have the *real* story for me? Snoop seems to think *you* are behind the floornappings, but I know you all like to snoop—except maybe for Miranda. I haven't seen her with this crew before." He looked straight at Jezabelle, indicating she should begin.

Jezabelle sighed. "We're trying to figure out a connection among our floors. We think it might be some kind of puzzle. Miranda found out that the Brilliant brothers loved puzzles and published books of puzzles back in the late 1800s, early 1900s. We think they carried their puzzle-making over to the building of the town."

"We'd agree with that," Hank continued, "but we haven't determined yet what they're looking for."

"That makes no sense," Mr. Warbler pointed out.

Phoebe moved over next to Hank, grabbed his arm, and moved in closely. "Of course, it does. Hank always makes sense, don't you Hank?" She looked up into Hank's face and batted her eyelashes.

The door opened again and Rock Stone entered the room.

"Rock what are you doing here?" Jezabelle asked.

"Police... Chief... Hardy... called... me... out of... work... for... questioning. Sadie... said I... should... come... right... in. She said... I also... might... want... to rescue... you."

"Stone, good of you to join us. Did you know what your neighbors were up to today?" Jeb Jardene nodded his head toward Jezabelle and her friends.

Rock Stone looked at his neighbors and turned to Hank. "No... I was... at... work all... day."

Hank nodded. "That's fine. You're all free to go." Hank held the door open and indicated they all should leave.

"Just like that, we can go?" Jezabelle asked suspiciously.

"We can fly the coop?" Mr. Warbler was skeptical.

"Oh, Hanky, I knew you wouldn't keep us here much longer. Do you want to come over for some whipped cream?" Phoebe winked at Hank.

Lizzy said nothing but yanked Phoebe out of the room.

Miranda, being the last to leave, stopped in front of Hank. "What are you up to?"

Hank smiled at Miranda. "What comes up must come down."

CHAPTER TWENTY-NINE

The Brilliant BeDazzle Brewery was packed when the group entered. Rock Stone raised his hand at someone across the room and the person pushed through the crowd of people standing in line for the wine tasting to greet Rock.

"Rock, my boy!" The man shook Rock's hand. "And who do we have here? I thought the meeting was just between us."

Rock glanced behind him at the group, seeing suspicion on their faces.

Before Rock could answer, Jezabelle pushed Rock out of the way. "And you are?" She held out her hand to the stranger.

"Fleck Flaherty, real estate agent." He grabbed Jezabelle's hand in a firm grasp.

Jezabelle turned to Rock. "You're selling your house?"

"No. But... Fleck... and I... go way... back. I thought... I would ask... him about... Annabelle's... house... and see... if... he remembered... her... floor or... had any... pictures."

"But I didn't know I was meeting with all you prestigious people. Aren't you the famous Penderghast Puzzle Protectors? I saw your picture on the front page of the newspaper this morning." Fleck Flaherty mimicked taking their picture with an imaginary camera.

"I... was... meeting... them here... at... ten o'clock after... our... meeting. I was... going to... show... them... what you... described... to me," Rock explained.

"I'll show you all at the same time. What do you think of my place here?" Flaherty turned and made a sweep of the room with his arm, pride lining his face.

"You own this place and are a real estate mogul?" Phoebe came forward and took Fleck's arm. "How do you do it all?" she purred.

Jezabelle and Lizzy looked at each other, rolling their eyes. "Suppose you tell us what you were going to tell Rock," "Miranda suggested.

"Better yet, I'll show you. Come back to my office." Fleck took Phoebe's arm and led the way.

The group noticed the beautiful design of the new building. It looked like it had been built at the same time the rest of Brilliant had been established. The walls were decorative brick, tin tiles lined the high ceilings, the woodwork looked original, and the floors were old stone brick. Back in Fleck's office, the old-time style continued and old framed photos lined the wall.

"You certainly kept the character of the town when you built this new building," Mr. Warbler remarked, inspecting the stained glass window in the office.

"Most of what you see is salvage bought at salvage stores and some found in basements here in Brilliant or from buildings that were torn down here in town during the past few years," Fleck explained. He pointed to some pictures on the wall. "Here's Annabelle Avary's house."

The group gathered around the pictures. "Where did you get these?" Jezabelle asked, peering closely at the photographs of the inside of Annabelle's house.

"They were in her attic and when her daughter cleaned out the attic after Annabelle passed, she found them and threw them in the dumpster. Since I was the real estate agent for the house and working on this building, I snooped in the dumpster to see if there was anything I could use. These pictures were too beautiful to throw away, so I picked them up for my office. I like to pretend this is my ancestor's home. It makes me feel a connection to the original town of Brilliant."

"Look! Here's the floor!" Miranda pointed to a picture.

"Can you make out the square piece of the floor?" Warbler asked.

"I... brought... a... spyglass. I... thought... it was... perfect... for our... spying." Rock held the magnifying glass close to the picture.

"It looks like a picket fence," Phoebe stated.

"A picket fence with flowers!" Miranda's excitement showed in her voice. "I left the paper with my sketches in your living room, Phoebe. We have to add this to the picture. Maybe we can figure it out now because we seem to have all the pieces."

"So what's this all about?" Fleck asked Rock.

"Just... a little... party... game, putting... the... pieces... of the... puzzle together... for a... prize," Rock answered, not looking at Fleck so he didn't give it away that he was stretching the truth.

Fleck reached behind his desk and pushed a button. A bookshelf swung in and revealed another room. "This is my wine room with my private stock." He walked into the room, ignoring the astonished looks of his guests. Grabbing a bottle off one of the racks, he came back out and handed it to

Phoebe. "Take this home and enjoy the rest of the night."

Phoebe, not knowing what to say, blushed. "Ah, thank you."

"It's a bribe." Fleck winked at Phoebe.

"A bribe?" She looked at Jezabelle. "A bribe?"

Fleck laughed. "Yes, a bribe so that you'll come back one night and let me buy you dinner."

Relief was evident in Phoebe's voice. "Oh, that kind of a bribe."

Looking confused, Fleck said, "What kind of a bribe did you think I meant?"

Jezabelle, seeing things were getting out of hand and worried Phoebe would blurt out what they were really doing, grabbed Phoebe's arm and marched her out of the office, turning back to Fleck to comment, "A bribe is a bribe unless you're a bride."

The rest of the group rolled their eyes at the comment and followed after Phoebe and Jezabelle, all except for Rock. He shrugged his shoulders, turned to Fleck, and said, "Don't ask, don't tell, with Jezabelle things don't always jell."

CHAPTER THIRTY

Since none of the group except for Rock had a
vehicle, Rock took turns driving the group home
from downtown Brilliant. It was only a mile and
they could have walked, but it had been a long day
and their neighborhood was on the edge of town
with old-fashioned streetlights that made it darker at
night. They had all concurred that, since there was a
floornapper around their neighborhood, perhaps a
ride would be best.

Jezabelle and Phoebe were the first two to be
dropped off. "Drop the others off at Phoebe's and
then come on over," Jezabelle instructed Rock.
"We're working late tonight."

"No baking tonight, Jezabelle?" Phoebe inquired
as they walked up to her house. "Why do you bake
every night?"

"It's something I like to do. It relaxes me. What
do you suppose we'll find when we put the pieces
together?" Jezabelle changed the subject.

Unlocking the door and stepping into the house,
Phoebe answered, "We'll find someone has been
here!"

Jezabelle looked in the direction Phoebe was
pointing—her living room. It had been ransacked,
and the drawing that Miranda had made was in tiny
little pieces on the floor.

Jezabelle picked up the pieces of the drawing
and looked around. "It appears this room and the
sunroom are the only two rooms they touched."

A gasp was heard from the doorway as Lizzy arrived and took in the scene. "What happened?"

Miranda moved into the living room. "Warbler will be here soon. Rock said he can't make it and we should keep him informed. Something about his beauty sleep." She walked into the sunroom and leaned down to touch the square of floor they had taken up.

"Should we call the police?" Lizzy asked.

Jezabelle's serious look told them she was pondering what they should do. "Maybe the police did this. Maybe that's why they kept us at the station all day and that fire story and chase was just to throw us off."

"You're saying we can't trust the police and Hank Hardy?" Mr. Warbler entered the house overhearing the conversation.

"Now what?" Lizzy sat down on the couch, discouraged. "We don't know who we can trust."

"Maybe you should ask Hank if they were the ransackers, Jezabelle, since you were sweet on each other a long time ago and he still watches out for you. He might confess," Phoebe suggested

Jezabelle shook her head. "Not until we know what we don't know. We have to be very careful. At least there don't appear to be any more dead bodies in our houses. Maybe Fred Rally's death was an accident."

"Phoebe, I need more paper and a pen. I'll redo my drawing and we'll go over what we know." Miranda sat down determined to recreate what they'd lost. "Drat, they took the bible verse too!"

Phoebe dug in her desk, came out with a tablet, and handed it to Miranda.

"First three boxes had *faith, hope,* and *love* on them." Miranda drew the squares.

"No, stop! It's charity," Jezabelle commented.

Miranda redrew the squares and put the corrected names on the squares. She then drew a hedge around the squares.

"Add my tree!" Warbler advised.

Miranda drew a tree in the back of the boxes. "What about what Fleck showed us? The square at Annabelle's house? It looked like a picket fence with flowers. Where do I put that?"

"Around the boxes and draw it farther down from the boxes to make it look like it's framing a square," Mr. Warbler suggested.

Miranda continued drawing and when she was done, she held it up. "What does that look like?"

"A private cemetery!" Lizzy guessed.

"Or maybe graves in the Brilliant Blessings' Cemetery!" Phoebe added.

"Why would someone steal our floor to put this together as a puzzle?" Jezabelle thought aloud.

"For the treasure?" Mr. Warbler questioned.

Lizzy turned to her friends. "After all this time, someone thinks there's a treasure? This was laid out over one hundred years ago and someone just decided to solve it now? Why? How did they know about it?"

Jezabelle turned to Miranda. "And if so, why did the Brilliant brothers leave your house out of the loop?"

Miranda shook her head. "Well, I have secret nooks and crannies. Maybe my house has the *answer* to the puzzle, although I keep turning up new things when I'm searching. I haven't found anything of value or that would help us. They're just quirky fun things that make you laugh. Sometimes there are little notes to what must have been the children of whichever brother lived in my house. I was told by my realtor—not Fleck—that that particular Brilliant brother had seven kids and he was always coming up with ways to tease them. Although I think it's strange that no one having lived in the houses since that time, and before us, was not snoopy enough to search out the fun surprises."

"You're the mystery writer, Miranda, so you're always looking for a mystery so the story intrigued you. Or maybe the realtor before the one you had never told anyone about the history of the house," Jezabelle suggested.

"I'm tired." Mr. Warbler looked at the bird watch on his arm. "My birds and squirrels are going to be up mighty early. Can we continue this conversation sometime tomorrow? We don't seem to be solving anything tonight." He yawned.

"Phoebe, you forgot to uncork your wine. Saving it for your dinner with Fleck?" Jezabelle teased. "I agree with Warbler. Let's call it a night. Good night, all!" Jezabelle moved toward the door.

"I'm going out the sunroom door; it's closer," Miranda stated.

"How am I going to get home?" Lizzy worried. "I don't have a car."

"Come on, Lizzy, it's two o'clock in the morning. You might as well stay with me. I have some perfect Mickey Mouse pajamas you can borrow." Jezabelle grabbed her arm and pulled her toward the door.

"Good night." A yawning Warbler followed the women.

"Night all! Sleep tight and don't let the floornappers bite!" Phoebe hollered after them.

Once outside, Warbler sprinted as fast as his heavy body could carry him over to his house.

Jezabelle and Lizzy walked, arm in arm, across the street. They reached Jezabelle's veranda when they heard a car coming down the street. They ducked into the shadows of the roof overhang. A car turned into Rock's driveway. Without being seen by the driver, the two women moved to the side of the porch so they could see Rock's backyard. A woman got out of the vehicle, opened the garage door, and put the car in Rock's garage. They watched her move from the garage to the house and heard her lightly tap on Rock's back door. They heard the door open and saw a light. Soon the light went out and all seemed quiet next door.

Jezabelle turned to Lizzy. "Who do you trust?"

CHAPTER THIRTY-ONE

Lizzy was lying in the bed in Jezabelle's spare bedroom, staring at the ceiling, when Jezabelle knocked on her door to offer her a cup of coffee. "Lizzy, are you awake?"

"I am. I've been contemplating our puzzle." She sat up on the bed and took the coffee from Jezabelle.

"I can't believe you wanted to sleep in the room with the plywood over the hole in the floor. There are three other bedrooms you could have chosen." Jezabelle eyed the plywood square. "I'm not sure how I'm going to fix this so it will look good again."

"We find the pieces and put them back," Lizzy said firmly. "By the way, is it just me? When I lay in bed and look at the rest of the floor, it looks like there's an *M* at the west edge of the floor." She got out of bed and walked across the room. "See!" Lizzy pointed at the edges and followed the end pieces of the floor.

Jezabelle studied what Lizzy was doing. Frowning, she put her coffee cup down and stood by Lizzie. "It does, doesn't it? These two pieces make a pattern, coming down like the middle of the *M*."

"Do you suppose it's a fluke or part of the puzzle?" Lizzy asked.

"Why an *M*?" Jezabelle wondered.

"Let's go see if Warbler has a letter on his floor or if we're imagining things." Lizzy opened the closet door to get her clothes. "Go and get dressed. We're losing time."

"Lizzy, it's six in the morning. Warbler won't even be up yet."

"We'll get him up." Lizzy pulled on her shirt and pushed Jezabelle out the door toward her bedroom.

Jezabelle yelled across the hallway to Lizzy as Lizzy was looking for her shoes. "I hear the garbage truck. Hick is really early today. I better get my garbage."

"I'll get it!" Lizzy offered. "I'm dressed. Meet you outside!"

Jezabelle finished pulling on her clothes, took another sip of her coffee, and then slowly traversed the stairs. The two friends had stayed up past two o'clock and now they were up at six. *She and Lizzy were getting too old for this,* she thought.

Stepping outside onto her porch, Jezabelle saw the owner of the Brilliant Junk Yard Garbage Company picking up her trash. She hurried to talk to him before he left. "Chatfield, where's Hick?"

"He didn't show up for work this morning. First time that's ever happened; wasn't answering his phone either. He better have a good excuse for this. He's a good guy but burning too many candles. Probably fell asleep on his other job. See you, ladies!"

Jezabelle and Lizzy watched the garbage truck move down the street. "I wonder what happened?" Jezabelle's face puckered up in concern.

"We'll figure that out later. Let's go get Warbler." Lizzy ran across the street and rang Warbler's modern doorbell.

When Jezabelle caught up to Lizzy, Mr. Warbler was answering the door. "What... what... are my squirrels dead? Is there a fire?"

"Relax, Warbler, we want to inspect the floor in your bedroom." Jezabelle moved past him and put her foot on the stairs.

"You want to look at my plywood?" Mr. Warbler wrinkled his nose.

"No, the rest of your floor. Let's go!" Lizzy grabbed Warbler's arm and pulled him toward the stairs. "Follow Jezabelle!"

When they reached Warbler's room, Lizzy let go of his arm. "What did you do to this room?" Lizzy asked in disbelief, seeing the disarray of the furniture.

"I moved the furniture around so if someone wanted to steal more of my floor they'd have to move the furniture first. See this line right here?" Warbler reached up to show them a string.

"Yes?" Both Jezabelle and Lizzy spoke at the same time.

"It's hooked to a camera and if anyone moves any of the furniture, it's going to click on the camera mounted to the ceiling."

"Well, it's going to have to click away, although I think if we moved the furniture that weak string is just going to break," Lizzy informed him.

"Why are we moving the furniture?" Warbler asked.

"So we can find a clue." Jezabelle pushed on the wardrobe that was in the middle of the floor. "Help me move this!"

Warbler and Jezabelle pushed the wardrobe to the side of the room.

"Let's move these other pieces into the middle of the room too and see if we can see anything," Jezabelle suggested, pushing on a desk.

The trio moved the furniture to the right side of the room so they could get a good look at the floor.

"There it is! See that!" Jezabelle pointed to the floor. Part of what she saw was covered by the nightstand. She moved over to the nightstand and gave it a shove.

Lizzy looked down at the floor that had been partially covered by the nightstand. "It's not as big as yours, Jezabelle."

Warbler stared at the floor. "What is it?"

Jezabelle walked around the design, contemplating what she was seeing. "It looks like it's a *U*."

"So what does it mean?" Lizzy inquired.

"I don't know," Jezabelle answered. We have an *M* and a *U*."

"*MU?*" Do you suppose it's another way to spell *mew* as in the way a cat sounds?" Warbler guessed.

"Since the Brilliant brothers were puzzle makers, do you suppose this is a piece of our puzzle or a new one?" Lizzy wondered.

"If I remember right, my house was built first," Jezabelle informed her friends. "And Warbler's house was built second. Phoebe's was third, Rock's fourth, Annabelle's fifth and Miranda's last. Let's go see what's at Phoebe's house. Remember we all thought her sunroom floor was strange." Jezabelle moved toward the door.

"I've got to get dressed," Warbler stated.

Jezabelle and Lizzy were so excited about finding another piece of the puzzle they hadn't looked at what Warbler was wearing. His statement made them turn and look at him. They both burst out laughing.

"What so funny?" Warbler's miffed tone made them laugh harder.

"We're... sorry, uh, hmm, but we didn't know you liked Batman and we didn't know they made batman pajamas for someone as... as... well proportioned as you," Jezabelle noted. "We'll meet you at Phoebe's."

Jezabelle and Lizzy left the house, still trying to rein in their laughter.

Mr. Shifty and Mrs. Mysterious greeted them when they reached Phoebe's front porch. "They must have had an early morning romp with Jasper and Max. They weren't home last night. I think I'm going to have to put in a kitty door so they can get in and out by themselves," said Jezabelle, ringing Phoebe's doorbell.

When Phoebe didn't answer, Lizzy pounded on the door. Mr. Warbler joined them.

"We could throw rocks at her bedroom window." Warbler left the porch and picked up some rocks from the flower garden.

"Maybe something happened to her." Lizzy's worried voice suggested what they all were thinking.

"We made enough noise to wake the dead," Jezabelle concluded and then, realizing what she'd said, clamped her hand over her mouth.

Mr. Warbler hurried to the side of the house, yelling back them, "I know where she keeps the key hidden!"

Jezabelle and Lizzy followed Warbler to the back of the house. He reached under a bush, picked up a rock, and came up with a key.

"It's the back door key; come on!" He motioned them to follow him.

Warbler was about to put the key into the lock when Lizzy said, "Do you suppose we should go in like this or should we call Hank?"

Jezabelle grabbed the key out of Warbler's hand, inserted it in the lock, and turned it until they heard the latch open. She stuck her head in the door. "Yoo Hoo!" There was no answer. Jezabelle moved cautiously into the kitchen. Lizzy and Warbler followed.

"The kitchen looks like it always does—very clean," Warbler stated, taking in the pristine kitchen.

"Yah, she's not much for cooking. Has other people do it and brings it in," Jezabelle explained to Lizzy.

"Maybe she's gone," Lizzy whispered.

"Why are you whispering?" Jezabelle asked. "If she's gone, she can't hear you and if she's dead she can't hear you either."

"Jezabelle, is that any way to talk?" Mr. Warbler chastised her. "Now what?"

"Well, we could look at her floor and leave or we can see if she's somewhere in this house," Jezabelle suggested.

"If she's here and something's wrong we can't just leave." Lizzy looked toward the stairs in the living room.

"Lizzy and I will see if she's upstairs. Warbler, you stay here in case we need you to call for help for us." Jezabelle looked around the kitchen. She walked over and opened a drawer, nodding in satisfaction at what she found. She reached into the drawer and pulled out a large fork and a butcher knife. She handed the fork to Lizzy while keeping the butcher knife for herself.

"What about me?" Mr. Warbler jumped up and down nervously on his toes shaking the floor.

"Warbler, these old houses are fragile. Be still! You have the door. If you get scared, call and run for help and remember—we actually love you and like you." Jezabelle nodded to Warbler while grabbing Lizzy's arm, moving her toward the stairs.

Slowly, they held on to each other and climbed the stairs. "What do we do if we find her dead?" Lizzy stumbled on the word *dead* and Jezabelle had to grab her to keep her from falling. She didn't answer Lizzy's question.

Once upstairs, they checked the first bedroom. "Must be a guest room," Jezabelle guessed.

Holding on to each other for comfort, they came to the second bedroom. The door was open and there was Phoebe on the bed. They both stared before Lizzy whispered, "Someone blindfolded her and murdered her." She held up her fork in front of her.

Jezabelle moved into the room standing above Phoebe's prone figure. "There's no blood." She laid her knife down on the floor.

"Does she have a pulse?" Lizzy grabbed Jezabelle's arm and moved it to Phoebe's neck so Jezabelle could feel for a pulse. Jezabelle's arm touched Phoebe's neck.

Phoebe's prone body sat straight up in bed. "What? Who? What are you doing here? You scared the life out of me! Who are you? Have you come to steal my floor? Hasn't anyone told you about doorbells? What time is it?"

Jezabelle was down on the floor holding Lizzy who had fainted when Phoebe, thought to be a corpse, sat up in bed.

"What's going on up there?" Warbler's voice yelled from the bottom of the steps. "Is she dead?"

"Lizzy or Phoebe?" Jezabelle yelled back.

"What?" Warbler's heavy tread could be heard on the stairs.

"Phoebe, we did ring the doorbell and knocked too," Jezabelle informed the woman on the bed, while gently tapping Lizzy's face to wake her up.

"What?" Phoebe tore the black sleep mask off her face, reached to her ears, then pulled an earplug out of each ear. "It's you! You scared me half to death! I can't see or hear anything with my sleep mask on and my earplugs in. How did you get in here?"

Phoebe turned as Warbler entered the bedroom. "You showed them where the key is, didn't you? Didn't you? That key was only for emergencies! Again I ask, what are you doing here?"

Lizzy woke up in time to hear the last question. "We thought you were dead. We came to see if you have part of the puzzle."

Jezabelle stood up and stuck out her hand to help Lizzy up. "We thought when you didn't answer your doorbell that you might be in trouble, so don't be mad at Warbler. We thought it might be an emergency and the floornapper got you."

"Glad you're okay but we have to look at your floor," Warbler explained. "Jezabelle has an *M* and I have a *U*."

Phoebe threw her blankets off her body to reveal what looked to be an expensive pair of silk pajamas, lapels lined with what the others' assumed were rhinestones. She glanced at the clock beside her bed. "Do you realize it's only six-thirty? This better be a breakthrough because you interrupted my beauty sleep."

Mr. Warbler was already down the stairs and on the way to the sunroom. The others followed him. The warm sun was shining into the window.

"Look right there!" Lizzy pointed to a spot in the floor.

"That's what you're looking for? You could have just asked. I have no idea why that design is there but it looks like they goofed when they bordered the floor. The edge on one side is straight and they angled the design corners and instead of bringing it up straight on the other side, it's kind of rounded. I always thought maybe I should hire some craftsman and fix it." Phoebe made her feelings of her frustration with the design known.

"It's a *D*. It's a *D*!" Lizzy jumped up and down shouting the letter.

Phoebe sat down. "Too early for cheerleading, Lizzy. You weren't a cheerleader in high school, were you?

"No, what she means is the letter *D*. We now have *M-U-D*. But what does it mean?" Jezabelle sat down next to Phoebe, staring at the floor.

"*Mud*? They liked to play in the *mud*?" Mr. Warbler guessed.

"Should we call the others or Hank?" Lizzy had her phone in her hand.

"Let's check out Rock's house and see if he has any letters. If Lizzy hadn't slept at your house last night we wouldn't know about this," Mr. Warbler commented.

"Yes, and we know *so* much about this," Jezabelle sarcastically suggested. "And I have a feeling this is just the beginning of what we know about nothing."

CHAPTER THIRTY-TWO

Jezabelle was the first to reach Rock Stone's house. She raised her hand and tapped hard on the back door.

"Maybe ringing the old crank bell would help?" Lizzy suggested while turning the nob to ring the bell on the old-fashioned doorbell.

"Do you supposed he's at work already? It's past seven. Maybe we should call him?" Phoebe pulled her cell phone out of her pocket.

"You have his number?" Jezabelle asked.

Frowning, Phoebe answered, "Well—no."

Jezabelle smiled. "I do." She reached in her pocket and pulled out her cell phone. "Rock Stone." She listened as the phone rang. Ending the call, she turned to the others. "No answer. No problem. I still have the key. I'll run home and get it." She turned to walk over to her back porch.

"Will we get arrested?" Mr. Warbler whispered to Lizzy.

Lizzy thought for a moment. "Well, technically it's not breaking and entering if we have the key."

They watched Jezabelle trekking back to where they stood, key in hand. She handed it to Mr. Warbler. "Open the door."

He handed the key back. "I'm not opening the door; you open the door. Then they'll arrest you, not me, for breaking and entering."

"Well, Warbler," Jezabelle said while opening the door with her key, "they'll get us all for trespassing. Which is the tougher sentence?" She chuckled as she stepped into the kitchen.

"At least, it's daylight and we don't need to turn on any lights. Yoo hoo!" Phoebe yelled, walking further into the house and standing by the staircase. Not hearing an answer, she said to the others, "The coast is clear."

Jezabelle led the way up the stairs to the bedroom. They stepped into the room to gaze at the floor.

Mr. Warbler shook his head. "I don't see any letters."

"Maybe it's hidden by the bed." Lizzy got down on her hands and knees and peered under the bed. Her hand disappeared and she came out with a woman's bra. "Well, something's under the bed but it's certainly not a letter." She twirled the bra over her head.

"Maybe it belongs to the mysterious car that keeps disappearing in his garage around two in the morning." Jezabelle raised her eyebrows.

Phoebe's eyes stretched open as wide as they could at the statement.

"Watch it, Phoebe. I can tell you're going to start with the who and *now* is not the time. Let's move some furniture and see if we see anything. Make sure we put everything back so we don't have to tell him we were ever here."

"There's nothing here," Miranda stated. "So maybe all we need for the puzzle is *MUD*."

"Let's check the other houses to make sure," Jezabelle suggested. Her phone vibrated in her pocket. "Who'd be calling me so early in the morning? It's Miranda. Shouldn't she be sleeping?"

"So should we," Phoebe reminded Jezabelle.

They all heard Miranda's excited voice shouting on the other end of Jezabelle's phone, "I found it! I found it! Are you up? I'll be right over!"

"No!" order Jezabelle, "You stay where you are! We'll be right over and, yah, we're up!"

CHAPTER THIRTY-THREE

Miranda was waiting with her door open ready to usher the group into her house. "You must have all been together. Didn't you sleep all night either?"

"You didn't sleep all night? We slept—that is, I slept until I almost got scared out of my life early this morning when these three broke into my house!" Phoebe informed Miranda.

"I sleep odd hours so it's not big deal for me to be up all night, but I had a mission. You broke into her house?" asked Miranda to the group.

Jezabelle looked past Miranda into the living room and noticed things tossed hither and yon. "Did someone break into your house?"

Miranda answered, waving a piece of paper in the air. "I found it! I found it! Exactly what we need to help solve this puzzle! And it was right under my feet all the time!"

Jezabelle grabbed the old yellowed piece of paper and unfolded it. The others gathered around. "It's the original plat map that was carved in the wall at the library," explained Miranda.

"I thought no one was supposed to make a paper copy of that. It's in the bylaws of Brilliant," Lizzy reminded the group.

"Yes, but if the Brilliant brothers were the ones who drew it up in the first place, they certainly had the right to make a copy of it. In fact, that's what they did—right on the wall of the library! They carved the only copy there was and hid the original in my house," Miranda explained.

"Where did you find it?" Mr. Warbler asked as he fingered the delicate paper.

"Right underneath my feet." Miranda indicated the group should follow her to the living room. "You remember we talked about these tiny corner squares? I pried them all up and this paper was underneath the one in the west corner, folded up tight and tiny."

"We have news too," Phoebe proudly announced. "We found letters in our floors!"

"Letters? As in the kind people write?" Miranda inquired.

Jezabelle answered for Phoebe, "Letters as in letters of the alphabet in the design of our floors. We think mine is an *M*."

"And mine is a *U*," Mr. Warbler added.

Phoebe piped up, "I have a *D*."

Miranda wrinkled her nose in thought. "*M-U-D*? *Mud*? What does that mean?"

"We have no idea. Rock Stone doesn't have a letter," Warbler interjected.

Jezabelle had her nose close to the map, studying the small writing. "It looks like there's a farm listed here on the map by the name of *Mud* but with two *D*s." They all leaned in close to see what Jezabelle had found.

"*Mudd* was someone's farm?" Mr. Warbler muttered. "We don't have a Mudd family around here now."

"Miranda does your house have another *D*?" Lizzy asked.

Miranda shook her head. "No *D* in this house; perhaps that's why the map was here. Mine was the last and most intricate and interesting house built on this block by the Brilliant brothers. I've been doing some research. Annabelle's house was built right before mine. Maybe she has the *D*. But why would they skip Rock's house?"

Jezabelle sat down in the rocking chair on the sun porch. "And what does it all mean? The pieces of the floor? The notes in between the floor? The letters on the floor? And the plat map?"

"That's a lot of puzzle pieces to put together," Lizzy concluded.

Mr. Warbler stood up straight, raised his hand in the air and said, "But we can do it! We're the Penderghast Puzzle Protectors and we're on a mission to save the floors of Brilliant and... maybe some people too!"

"Okay, Warbler, sit down and let's put these pieces together," Jezabelle suggested.

The rest of the group took a seat as Jezabelle continued, "First, someone stole Warbler's floor while he was ah, ah..." Seeing Mr. Warbler give her a warning look, she finished her statement, "out of the house."

"And we don't know if there was a paper underneath his floor because we don't have it, but what we do know is that there was a tree on his puzzle piece. And we also don't know whether Jezabelle had a note hidden under her floor, but we do know she had three boxes that look like tombstones." Lizzy added those details to the story.

"Underneath Rock's floor and my floor were papers with Bible verses so we could conclude that possibly those words were on a tombstone and the hedge might go around a cemetery plot. We have the letters *M-U-D* that were on our floors. Miranda found a plat map that has the name *Mudd* on it but with two *D*s. No Bible verses here." Phoebe heaved a sigh of relief; she'd gotten it all out in one breath.

Lizzy shook her head and then put her hands up to her temples. "I'm more confused than ever by all these clues. How do they connect? Why did Fred die? And where do we go from here?"

"Let's assume the other *D* is in Annabelle's house but we really don't need it," Jezabelle concluded.

Miranda was studying the map. This Mudd farm looks like it's not too far out of town. Does anyone know who owns this land now?"

Jezabelle peered over Miranda's shoulder. "That looks like it could be the old Darnel place. No one lives there now. It might be for sale."

Lizzy curiously studied her best friend while she said this, because Jezabelle's face and neck had a red tinge beginning to creep up and fill her normally pale skin. "Something wrong, Jezabelle?"

"Ah, no." Jezabelle cleared her throat, not wanting her friends to know that she'd just been out to that farm the other night.

"It's a beautiful day. I think we should go for a picnic on the farm," Lizzy suggested.

"Won't that be trespassing?" Mr. Warbler asked.

"If someone sees us, we just tell them we got lost looking for Butterfly Park so we could have a picnic," Phoebe plotted.

"Butterfly Park? Is that a new park? I've never heard of it," Lizzy stated.

Phoebe gave Lizzy a pointed look. "Neither has anyone else. Why do you think we got lost looking for it?"

Jezabelle laughed. "Picnic it is, but we need some food first. Let's stop at the Brilliant Bistro and pick up some picnic food."

At the word food Warbler hustled to the door and held it open indicating to the others they should exit, adding a word of advice before he closed the door behind them. "Do we all have our houses locked?" He rattled Miranda's doorknob making sure it was secure. "After all, our floornappers respect no boundaries and neither will we. Onward! Food!"

CHAPTER THIRTY-FOUR

Jiffy Jacks had his nose stuck in the oven when the group entered the Bistro. "Jiffy!" Jezabelle hollered to get his attention. The group could hear him muttering to himself as they stood at the counter.

Jiffy pulled his head out of the oven. "Sorry, I was doing a little cleaning. Can't be too careful, you know. What's up?"

"We need a picnic basket with sandwiches. You choose what kind and whatever fixings you have for a picnic." Jezabelle gave Jiffy the leeway to be creative.

"Where's the picnic?" Jiffy asked.

"We're going to Butterfly Park," Mr. Warbler answered.

A thoughtful look formed on John "Jiffy" Jacks' face. "Where's that? I've never heard of it."

Lizzy coughed. "Well, it's in an out-of-the-way spot. We may have to do some investigating to find it."

"Investigating? That sounds suspicious." Jiffy laughed. "In fact, all of you being together is suspicious. All of a sudden, you're all out and about and during the daytime too." He gave Miranda a pointed look.

Miranda gave a fake giggle. "I'm so loving the daytime. I never went out during the day until I met my neighbors and now I'm going on a picnic! Can you believe it?"

"No." Jiffy shook his head before looking at Jezabelle suspiciously. "Sweetie, are you sure this isn't part of the Penderghast Puzzle Protectors' Club and you aren't up to something? Maybe I should call Hank or Hanna. Maybe they'd want to go along."

"John 'Jiffy' Jacks, just get our food or it'll be dark before we get to our picnic. And just when did you get so suspicious?"

"I'll get your food and I hope you find Butterfly Park, but I warn you if Hank Hardy asks if I've seen you, I'll have to tell him the truth."

Jezabelle glared at Jiffy. "And why would he ask you about me?"

Jiffy got agitated. "Well, it might slip out if he comes in here."

Jezabelle pounded a fist on the counter. "Jiffy, if you say anything to Hank about me, you might be missing a few... donuts in the morning!"

Jiffy clamped his mouth shut, turned, and walked back into the kitchen to make their picnic.

Lizzy gave Jezabelle an inquiring look. "That last statement scared him. Why?"

"Well, you know sometimes he's two donuts short of a fruitcake." Jezabelle smiled and indicated they should all sit down and wait.

CHAPTER THIRTY-FIVE

Lizzy navigated the plat map while Jezabelle drove her Smart Car to the site of what was formerly the Mudd farm when Brilliant was founded.

Since Jezabelle's car had limited room, they had to take two cars. Miranda drove the second car, bringing Mr. Warbler and Phoebe with her.

Jezabelle already knew where the farm was, but she didn't want to let the others know she'd been there the other night.

"You found this rather easily," Lizzy remarked. "I didn't even have to give you too many directions. You seemed to know where to turn. Why's that?"

"Sixth sense, Lizzy. I have a sixth sense." Jezabelle stopped the car and stared at the scene ahead of her. "The house is gone! Burned down!"

Lizzy slowly got out of the car, staring at the charred ruins of what had been an old Victorian farm home. "Do you suppose it was a planned burn by the fire department? Didn't you say the owner had died? Maybe someone bought the property and burned down the house so they could build a new one."

The others joined Jezabelle and Lizzy. "No, this house was in beautiful shape. I ah... mean I heard it was in beautiful shape when I heard it was for sale." Jezabelle quickly covered her deceit.

"Maybe this is why we were stuck at the police station for so long. Didn't they say they had a house fire?" Miranda suggested.

"And we thought it was just a cover because your house was broken into, Miranda. Maybe the police were telling the truth."

"Enough speculating. Why are we here, Jezabelle?" Mr. Warbler broke up the conversation.

"We'll see if there's a cemetery on this land." Jezabelle turned around in a slow circle. She pointed behind the barn to the grove of trees. "Maybe it's behind those trees!"

Lizzy walked over behind the barn, calling out, "It looks like there might have been an old path here!"

"I'll get the picnic basket in case we find the site. We can have lunch there!" Mr. Warbler opened the trunk of Miranda's car.

"Eat at a cemetery?" Phoebe's eyes darted back and forth as she nervously twirled a piece of her hair.

"Afraid the ghosts might get your food, Phoebe?" Jezabelle teased. "We're coming Lizzy!"

They met up with Lizzy at the back of the barn. "Maybe we should bring our cars around to the back of the barn before we try to make it through that path," Miranda suggested. "There's room here for both cars and that way no one will know we're here."

"Good idea." Jezabelle threw her keys at Mr. Warbler. "Warby, will you move my car?"

Mr. Warbler turned to Miranda. "I don't think my rotund body will fit in Jezabelle's little car. I'll trade you keys."

Miranda handed her keys to Mr. Warbler and took Jezabelle's keys. They left the group to go move the cars.

Lizzy and Jezabelle moved to the path.

"It's going to be tough going. The path is pretty grown over but you can still see remnants of it. I wonder if the Darnels ever went back here." Lizzy tromped down some weeds.

"I don't think they did anything with the land. The house borders Rooster Pond and I guess they just used the barn for storing their antique cars. Mr. Darnel was quite a collector from the gossip I heard. I think that's why they bought the place. They lived here over fifty years. Bought the place when they were first married and when Mrs. Darnel died, Mr. Darnel stayed on until he died," Jezabelle explained as she stepped on more weeds on the overgrown path. "I didn't know them which was strange since this is such a small community."

Phoebe listened to their conversation as she watched for the cars so she could help them park in the tight spot. As the two cars slowly edged over the rough ground to the back of the barn, Phoebe began motioning left and right with her arms.

Mr. Warbler stuck his head out the window of Miranda's car. "Phoebe, get out of the way. With your arms flapping here and there, we might cut them off."

Phoebe jumped back just as Miranda revved the Smart Car around the corner. Parking behind the barn, Miranda got out of the little vehicle and remarked, "I'm going to have to get one of these. I feel like a kid again with my first car!"

"Are we ready?" Jezabelle asked.

Mr. Warbler picked up the picnic basket he'd set by the barn and hoisted it in the air. "Onward!"

The group picked their way through the weeds and the path, moving aside small trees but still seeing a semblance of a path. "Are you sure there's a cemetery out here?" Phoebe challenged as the brush and trees got denser. "We might get lost."

"No, I'm not sure, but why would we have all those clues and the word *MUD* end up on the plat map?" Jezabelle reminded them.

"That's *M-U-D-D* on the plat map. We only had one *D*," Phoebe stated.

"Phoebe!" Jezabelle cried, exasperated at Phoebe's thought processes, raised her voice, "We just didn't find the other *D*. It must be at Annabelle's house!"

Miffed at Jezabelle's tone, Phoebe answered, "Well, maybe we should have checked Annabelle's house before we traipsed all the way out here on a wild-goose chase!"

"It's a wild-goose chase all right." Mr. Warbler kept on going while the others were exchanging words. "Look!"

The three women scurried ahead, wanting to see what Mr. Warbler was pointing at. They came out in a small clearing by the far side of Rooster Pond that was full of geese.

"Wow! This side of the pond is really overgrown with weeds," Miranda said as they all huddled in the small clearing.

Jezabelle looked up at the tall brush to her left that was so dense you couldn't see through it. A thoughtful look on her face got the others' attention. She reached out and touched the brush. "Could this be an overgrown hedge?" she asked.

The others moved closer to study it. "It could be. How do we get through it if it is?" Miranda asked, touching the thick and prickly branches.

"Well, if it's a hedge, there has to be an opening." Lizzy began tramping through the weeds following the large perimeter of the hedge. Mr. Warbler followed Lizzy.

Jezabelle went in the other direction with Phoebe and Miranda following. She reached the edge and the turn of the bush, but it went right up to a few feet from the pond. Could she edge around it without falling in the pond?

"Let's take off our shoes and wade around," Miranda suggested. It looks muddy but not too deep right at the edge."

"You want us to wade in that murky water? There might be leeches." Phoebe peered into the water.

"I never met a leech I didn't like." Jezabelle took off her shoes and waded in. Miranda followed. After a few seconds, Phoebe, not wanting to be left behind, did the same.

As they stepped into the water, they saw Lizzy and Mr. Warbler doing the same thing further down, only Mr. Warbler was holding Lizzy's hand and Lizzy was giggling like a teenager.

When they finally all met on dry ground, they turned and all they could do was stare at each other before Phoebe broke the silence. "We did it! We did it! We solved the puzzled! We found it!" Phoebe jumped up and down with excitement.

Jezabelle reached out and grabbed her arm to stop her from jumping. "Yes, but we still don't know what the puzzle means." Jezabelle moved forward.

"Look! It looks just like the pieces of the puzzle. The crosses must have been plus signs to tell us to put the pieces together." Miranda pointed. "And look! There is what used to be a white picket fence! That must be Annabelle's piece."

"It's a little overgrown but there are the tombstones and my tree!" Mr. Warbler pointed to what was now a large oak tree behind the tombstones.

Jezabelle frowned and moved closer to the gravesite. "But look! There's freshly piled dirt by one tombstone."

Slowly, they moved forward taking in their surroundings.

"We must be in the right place because someone else was here not too long ago," Miranda guessed.

They walked over to the mound of dirt. They looked down and all gasped at the same time.

Jezabelle fell to her knees and reached down as far as she could into the dug grave. She touched the neck of the body lying in the grave. Looking up at the others, she barked, "Call an ambulance! He's still alive!"

Miranda crawled down into the grave with the barely breathing Hickory Rafferty while Phoebe called 9-1-1. She tapped Hick's face and listened to see if he was breathing. Lifting his head, she saw a large gash on the back of his head. "He has a head injury," she called up to the others.

"Warbler, Phoebe, go back to the barn and let the emergency crew know where we are," Jezabelle instructed.

As the two left, Miranda looked up at Jezabelle. "And how are we going to explain this?"

CHAPTER THIRTY-SIX

"It looks like we'll have to wait to interview Hick, so I guess we'll start with all of you." Hank looked Jezabelle straight in the eye. "What in tarnation are all of you doing out here? And how did you find this place?"

Jezabelle stuck her chin out. "HH, we were out for a picnic and it's good we decided to picnic here or we wouldn't have found poor Hickory."

"Yes." Lizzy came up and stood beside Jezabelle.

"Hank, haven't you ever wanted to go on a picnic?" Phoebe sidled up next to HH, hoping her charms would distract him.

"Ah, I wanted to bird watch and someone told me this was the best place." Warbler gave his explanation, stepping to Jezabelle's other side.

Miranda looked at the group. "It's like this. I accidently pulled up a piece of my floor last night when I was coming up with a plot line for my next book and I found this map. We decided to follow the map and see what we found and have a picnic too. Isn't it a beautiful day?"

Hanna joined the group. "Looks like Hick was digging a grave and someone clunked him on the back of the head."

Steve Straight hollered over from the open pit. "This is the only mound that's been touched! The others haven't been disturbed!"

Hank turned to the three trespassers. "Do any of you know why Hick was out here digging up an old gravesite?"

They all shook their heads.

Jezabelle decided it was time to let Hank in on what they knew; maybe Hick was the one doing the floornapping. "Can I have a minute with the Penderghast Puzzle Protectors?"

HH threw his hands up in the air in defeat. "Fine, but this better be good, Jezzy. Take a few minutes while I confer with Steve." Hank joined Steve over by the grave, indicating Hanna should do the same.

Jezabelle gathered the group around her. "I think we need to tell him. Maybe he'll share with us what he knows and it'll get us off the hook. Until Hick wakes up, we can't prove we didn't do this."

Phoebe's eyes grew wide and she whispered, "You don't think he thinks we'd do something like that to Hick?"

"Well," Miranda interjected, "if we thought he was the one stealing the pieces of your floor, the police might think you're guilty."

Mr. Warbler gave Miranda a scathing look. "*We* are guilty? *You're* here too!"

Miranda answered, "I'm here in the interest of a story and I didn't have a floor stolen."

Lizzy was peering at the burial site as the others were bantering blame back and forth. "Look! The grave that was dug up was Charity. That name is one of the ones in the Bible verse. Is it significant that it's the one that's empty—except for Hick's body?"

They all turned and stared at the three plots. When Hank, Hanna, and Steve caught them staring, they quickly turned back into their circle.

"Maybe Hick got interrupted and didn't have time to dig up the other resting place?" Lizzy suggested.

"But what happened to the body in that grave?" Jezabelle wondered.

"They'd have had a hard time getting a coffin with a body in it out of here with all the growth on the path," Miranda pointed out.

"Boat maybe? A canoe?" Warbler suggested.

Jezabelle shook her head. "I think this pond is too shallow for any type of boat. It's kind of a slew, the type for looks. Otherwise, why wouldn't the owners have discovered this old gravesite? If they'd have used boats on the pond, they'd have noticed it."

"How could the Darnels live here all those years and not know it's here?" Lizzy asked.

"Maybe they did, but didn't tell anyone. They kept to themselves. Maybe it wasn't important. Anyone who'd have remembered it's here is probably dead now and if it wasn't on any map, no one would know," Jezabelle concluded.

"That's enough whispering!" Hank and his deputies joined the group.

"We have something to tell you." Jezabelle looked Hank straight in the eye. "We, the Penderghast Puzzle Protectors, have been working to solve the puzzle of the death of Fred Rally and the heisting of parts of our hardwood floors."

Phoebe chimed in, "Yes, we know you're busy, so we thought we'd help."

Hank looked at his deputies. "Secure this crime scene." Turning to the five amateur sleuths, he continued, "As for all of you—down to the station! I'll follow you in, so you don't get lost."

"Can you call ahead and have Sadie bring in some donuts from the Brilliant Bistro or ice cream from the Creamy Cow to go with our picnic lunch that we never got to eat?" Warbler held up the picnic basket he still gripped tightly in his hand. "We don't want these sandwiches to go to waste!"

CHAPTER THIRTY-SEVEN

Sadie had coffee poured and ready for them in the back room of the Brilliant Police Station when they arrived. "When I heard you were coming back, I checked to see what our movie of the day was and if you're here long enough you can watch it. It's *The Great Escape,* but don't get any ideas."

Hank Hardy entered the room followed by his daughter Hanna, Jeb Jardene, and Stick Straight. He threw his notebook down on the table and sat down next to Jezabelle. "Now, let's get started," he said, nodding at Jezabelle. "You first, and the true story."

Jezabelle tilted her head and rolled her eyes. "Fine. We concluded that the pieces of floor in our houses were a puzzle put together by the Brilliant brothers. They actually had puzzle books published under the name Roosevelt Strong. Miranda found that out."

Hank nodded. "We'd concluded that the floor pieces were puzzles too."

Jezabelle frowned, turned, looked at the others, and turned back to Hank. "You didn't tell us that. We could have been in danger, at least those of us who still had floors." She chided her old friend.

"Go on with your story," Hanna interrupted Jezabelle.

Lizzy stood up. "I slept at Jezabelle's last night in the room that was floornapped. Lying in bed, I noted that the way the pattern in the hardwood floor was laid out, it seemed to have an *M* patterned into it."

"So Lizzy and Jezabelle woke me up and we discovered my hardwood floor had a *U* pattern," Warbler added.

"And they broke into my house, scared the living heck out of me when they woke me up and we discovered that I have a *D* pattern," Phoebe continued.

"But Rock Stone doesn't have anything on his floor. But he has the words *faith, hope* and *charity.*" Miranda broke in with her part of the tale. "And then I found the original plat map underneath one of the floorboards of my floor. And one of the farms shown on the map was a Mudd farm but with two *D*'s."

"But we don't know where the other *D* is. Maybe at Annabelle's but we didn't check yet," Phoebe added.

"All right, it's my turn," Hank broke in. "Where's Rock? If you were in his house and found he doesn't have a letter, he must be in on this too."

Silence greeted his question.

"Did he know you were in his house?" Hank asked.

"Kind of," Jezabelle finally answered.

"And what does that mean?" Jeb Jardene entered the conversation.

"I have his key." Jezabelle defended her actions. "I, ah, have to feed his cat when he's gone."

Phoebe piped up, "I didn't know he had a cat."

Jezabelle skewered Phoebe with her eyes.

"I, ah, yes, I seem to remember Giles—yes—Giles is his name. I'm sure." Phoebe agreed quickly.

"How long have you known about the puzzle caper?" Hank asked the group.

"Well, we finally put the pieces together this morning," Miranda answered. "And we followed the map to the farm."

"Do you realize that the farm is under an arson investigation? Someone burned down the house. That's why you were here so long before. And you could now be suspects in the arson case just by being found on the farm?" The sternness in Hank's voice was not lost on Jezabelle.

The door burst open and Jiffy Jacks pushed a cart into the room. "I heard you needed some dessert to go with your picnic basket. I didn't know you were having the picnic here. I thought you were going to Butterfly Park."

"Jiffy, we're conducting an investigation." Stick Straight stopped the cart before it came further into the room, pushing it back out and shutting the door.

Hank turned to Jezabelle. "Butterfly Park?"

Hanna wrinkled her nose in thought. "I've never heard of Butterfly Park."

"We were looking for it and we ended up where you found us. We thought it looked like Butterfly Park," Phoebe interjected.

Rock Stone opened the door and entered the room. "I... heard... you were... here... again. I... left... work... when I... heard... all of... you... were hustled... in here. Tom Burnside... said... Hick... was hurt... and I was... worried... about you. The... news is all... over... town."

"Speaking of Hick, Hank, have you heard how he is? Is he still alive? He barely had a pulse when we found him." Miranda's concern was echoed throughout the room.

"He's in a coma. Until he regains consciousness, he can't tell us what happened." Hanna answered for her father.

"Stone, you can take your neighbors home *again!*" Hank turned to the group, "Anything you forgot to tell me? Stay out of trouble. This is an active murder investigation. Fred Rally was murdered and it looks like someone tried to murder Hick. Or Hick is part of this. You could all be in danger. Jezzy, I don't want anything to happen to you or your neighbors."

"But Hank, that gravesite has something to do with the puzzle and we are the Penderghast Puzzle Protectors! You can't throw us off the case now!" Jezabelle implored Hank, feigning a wistful look.

"Jezzy, you were never *on* the case. Do you get that? There's more going on here than you know and it's for *us* to figure out." Hank turned toward Rock Stone. "Take them away! You seem innocent in this latest fiasco but, if I find out you're part of it, you'll end up in that jail cell, do you understand?"

Rock looked at Hank. "I... don't... want... to go... to... jail. I... will... watch... out for... them."

"We'll go. One thing though I have to ask." Jezabelle had a puzzled look on her face. "There was nothing in the grave that Hick was digging, or did someone steal whatever was in that grave? And is there anyone located in the other graves or are they empty too?"

Hank answered, "That's for *us* to know and you to find out only... *when* we have this crime solved!" He took Jezabelle's arm and led her over to the door, indicating the others should follow. "Oh, and Rock, take away the house key you gave her; she's been snooping in your house!"

Rock looked at Hank with an uncharacteristic twinkle in his eye. "But... who will... feed... Giles... when... I'm not... home?"

CHAPTER THIRTY-EIGHT

"It's almost suppertime; let's all walk over to The Brilliant BeDazzle Brewery and Wine Shop and get some supper and relax with a beer or a glass of wine. Maybe the pictures that Fleck has might show if there is a *D* on the floor," Jezabelle suggested. Then she turned to Rock. "And you don't have a cat by the name of Giles."

Rock grinned, something they hadn't seen him do before. "I... was... listening... outside the room... while... you were... explaining your... visit... to... my house. I... guess... I'm... going to... have... to... adopt... a cat and... name... him... Giles... to back up... your... story."

The group walked the couple of blocks to the new Brewery. Fleck Flaherty greeted the group when they walked in the door. "My favorite puzzle group! I heard you had a rough afternoon over at the police station. Supper's on me!" He laughed. "After all, it could be your last meal." He twitched his eyebrows at the statement.

Phoebe blushed and giggled when he finished the twitch with a wink in her direction.

Jezabelle poked Phoebe. "That sounded like a threat and you giggle?"

"He was joking Jezabelle—lighten up." Phoebe sat down at the table, looked around, then waved at someone across the room.

"It's Marion and Junior." Miranda waved too. "I wonder if Junior has our fake-them-out puzzle solved at the library."

"Warbler, cat got your tongue? You hardly said a word at the police station." Jezabelle pointed out.

"I, ah, was afraid I might incriminate myself." Warbler looked down at the floor.

Phoebe laughed. "Stealing bird feed from Rock?"

A blush rose on Warbler's face. "Ah, no—I have a confession to make." He looked first at Phoebe and then Miranda.

Miranda nodded. "Go ahead, Warbler. I told you it would come out."

"Does this have something to do with you cavorting all hours of the night with Miranda?" Jezabelle asked.

"Cavorting with me?" Miranda's loud protest could be heard across the Brewery. Heads turned to see what the commotion was.

Marion and Junior quickly left their table and moved across the room to the group. "We thought we'd join you. It seems you're having a lively discussion; we see each other all the time, and we're kind of bored. Marion pulled a chair over from the next table.

Junior put his hand in the air to summon a waiter. "Would you mind moving our food over to this table?"

Mr. Warbler clamped his mouth shut the minute the intruding diners joined their table. The others looked disappointed that Mr. Warbler hadn't spilled his secret before Marion and Junior descended on them. Miranda was staring daggers at Warbler.

Lizzy cleared her throat. "Yes, um, we were discussing the new name of the library. And

Miranda was just saying that she was cavorting and enjoying herself with an editor friend the other night and he thought the new name of the library, The Library of Lackadaisical Musings, was the perfect name and he would visit our community and do a live review of Miranda's new book at the library." She smiled at Miranda.

"What did you say the name of your new book was, dear?" Marion asked.

"*The Pot Sticker* and, speaking of pot stickers, I think I need to go and ask Fleck what he's sticking in the pot of soup we ordered. Excuse me." Miranda got up from the table in search of Fleck Flaherty.

Jezabelle, seeing Miranda head for the office instead of the kitchen, knew Miranda was seeking the pictures of Annabelle's house. Jezabelle turned to Junior to draw the others' attention. "So, Junior, have you figured out our puzzle yet?" she asked, referring to the real puzzle that was being put together in the Brilliant Brothers' Room.

With a gleam in his eye, Junior answered, "Yes, very interesting puzzle. Although, it lacks a few pieces that I haven't figured out yet. I should have it done by the end of the week. You should stop by and see it."

Jezabelle looked up just in time to see Jiffy Jacks entering the restaurant. Seeing the group, he headed for their table. "Jiffy, what are you doing here? Shouldn't you be baking at the Bistro for the morning rush?."

"Sweetie, I thought I might run into you here. I just delivered some pies and cheesecakes to the Senior Citizens' Center. I'm expanding my business and catering to other establishments now that I have this baking thing down."

Jezabelle glared at Jiffy.

"Will you be needing me again, Jiffy? I can help out if you want some sleep," Miranda offered.

Jiffy ignored Miranda and said, "This is quite a group; what are you talking about? Are you putting the pieces together about the floors? And why were you out at the Darnel farm? Did you see the house? The police are saying it's arson."

Lizzy came up behind Jiffy and, hearing his conversation, she broke in. "I'm sorry. We have to go. I forgot I left my purse at Jezabelle's and I need to take my medicine. Rock, can you take turns driving us home in your truck again?"

Jiffy looked at Jezabelle. "Sweetie, I can drive you home." He winked.

No one saw Hank Hardy come in the back door so they were all surprised when he joined the group too. Hearing Jiffy's proposal, he intervened. "I'll give Jezzy and Lizzy and Phoebe a ride if you give Warbler a ride, Stone."

Rock Stone, having been silent throughout their visit to the Brewery, stood up. "I... can... do... that. Anything... to keep... the... chief... of police... on... my good... side."

Marion looked at Jiffy. "You can join us, Jiffy. We're not quite finished with our dinner, and it looks like these folks never even ordered."

"We just came here for the atmosphere," Phoebe blurted out.

"Well, I was going to buy and my wallet's in my purse at Jezabelle's," Lizzy explained.

"And we were full from that picnic dinner we ate while we were at the police station." Warbler grabbed Jezabelle's arm and hustled her out of the Brewery. The rest followed but not before Fleck hollered a good-bye across the brewery from outside his office.

Lizzy looked back at Fleck. "He's such an informative man."

"Don't you mean formative?" Phoebe asked.

Lizzy shook her head. "No I mean informative." She whispered in Phoebe's ear. "I have information."

CHAPTER THIRTY-NINE

Hank pulled into Jezabelle's driveway. Lizzy and
Phoebe exited the car and walked up to Jezabelle's
porch. Jezabelle opened the car door and was about
to follow Lizzy and Phoebe when Hank grabbed her
arm. "Jezzy, you need to be careful. We'll drop off
your cars later after we've checked them out and are
sure you aren't hiding anything to do with the
crime." He was about to say more when Phoebe and
Lizzy hurried up to the car. Lizzy was carrying a
large vase filled with a dozen red roses.

"Jezabelle, these were on your porch! There's a
card!" She thrust the vase, roses, and card into
Jezabelle's arms.

Hank raised an eyebrow. "Yes, Jezabelle, read
the card."

Jezabelle looked at the roses, glanced at Hank,
then opened the card.

"What does it say? What does it say?" Phoebe
grabbed the card out of Jezabelle's hand. "It says,
*Sweetie, Roses are Red, Violets are blue, I couldn't
be more in love with you.*" Phoebe's mouth dropped
open. "You have a boyfriend."

"I have to go. I have a crime to solve. Jezabelle,
I'll leave you to your roses." Turning to Phoebe and
Lizzy, Hank advised, "Don't let her smell too many
of them. Remember, the thorn is on the rose."

Jezabelle got out of the car and turned to Hank.
"But the rose knows." Turning to her two friends

she said, "Come on in; I see Rock is pulling in next door with Warbler. Let's have a nightcap."

Jezabelle had a glass of wine poured for each of them by the time Warbler and Rock Stone joined them.

"Can't... stay... long... I have... a... long... day ahead... of me... at... work since... I... left... early... today... and I... have to... get some... shut-eye."

"By the way, Rock, you've never told us what you do," Miranda asked.

Rock's hand was halfway to his mouth with his wine when the glass slipped out of his grasp and fell to the floor. He quickly got up, knocking into Mr. Warbler who was sitting next to him, knocking Mr. Warbler's glass to the floor too. "Oh... no look... what I've... done. It's... a... ... good... thing it's... white... wine."

Jezabelle grabbed a towel and handed it to Rock so he could soak up the wine. As he was working on the spot, he asked Miranda, "What... did you... see... when you... went... back to... the... office to... look... at the... pictures... at the... Brewery?"

"That's what I was so excited to tell you. Annabelle did have a big *D* around the edges of her floor. And at the edge of the big *D* it looked like there was maybe a rainbow and then on the bottom of the D was a bar."

"A bar? As in the type of bar you drink at?" Mr. Warbler asked.

"No, like a bar of soap, a candy bar, a bar of gold!" Miranda exclaimed.

"We know that the puzzle leads us to the Mudd family farm. We know that someone hired Hick to dig up a grave," Phoebe stated.

"Or, I hate to say it, Hick decided on his own to dig up the grave. He was familiar with our houses. Could he be the floornapper?" Jezabelle pondered the question.

"We didn't tell the police about the notes we found in the floors." Mr. Warbler jumped up, cell phone in hand.

"Sit back down, Warbler," Jezabelle ordered. "I didn't tell them on purpose. It's a part of our puzzle. We found that clue."

Miranda paced the room. "What do the Bible verses have to do with the puzzle?"

"The hedge was protection for the graves. But what about the *faith, hope* and *charity*?" Mr. Warbler asked.

"Well, Hick was digging up the grave of Charity. That was one of the names on the tombstones of the graves. We have to find out what the names of the wives or children of the Brilliant brothers were. We need to go back to the library and the Brilliant Brothers' Room. Their names would be there," Jezabelle informed the group.

"But the fact that they were authors of puzzle books must never have been found there or we would have heard about it," Phoebe reminded the group. "So maybe there will be names missing too."

"We... need... a plan... of... action... but I... have... to... leave... now. You... come... up... with... it... and... let me... know." Rock looked at Jezabelle. "You... have my... number... and my... key." With a twinkle in his eye, he added, "And... don't forget... to... feed... Giles." He put his wine glass down and walked out the door.

"That was quick," Lizzy surmised.

"He's right. We need a plan," Jezabelle stated. "It's getting late and I, ah, have things to do and then I need to get my old person sleep. Miranda, I suggest you see if you can find anything about the Brilliant Brothers' wives on the Internet. Then the Penderghast Puzzle Protectors will visit the library to work on our puzzle. Lizzy you might as well stay the night again."

"I've an idea," said Lizzy. "I'll call Fleck. I think he kind of likes me and I'll tell him I'm looking for a house for my sister to buy and I want to look at Annabelle's house. You can all come along to give your opinion. We'll take a close look at the *D* and whatever the rainbow-looking thing is."

Jezabelle frowned, "Lizzy, you don't have a sister."

"I know that but Fleck doesn't.

CHAPTER FORTY

Jezabelle dropped Lizzy at her house the next morning so she could pick up her car. Jezabelle continued on to the Brilliant Library while Lizzy visited The Brilliant Bedazzle Brewery and Wine Shop and Fleck Flaherty. Now that Fleck owned the Brewery and Wine Shop, he'd moved his real estate office there. Lizzy was house hunting.

Phoebe, Miranda, and Mr. Warbler were waiting outside the library for Jezabelle.

"Where's Lizzy?" Mr. Warbler asked, looking behind Jezabelle to see if Lizzy was still in the parking lot.

"She's visiting Fleck and doing some house hunting. Hopefully we'll hear from her so we can visit Annabelle's house," Jezabelle answered. She led the way into the library through the Hole in the Wall door to the Brilliant Brothers' Memorial Room. Junior was sitting at the table.

"Junior, we didn't expect to find you here." Phoebe gave him a suspicious look.

Junior smiled at the group. "Almost finished with this puzzle. Now can I join your group? I've proven I know how to put puzzles together."

"We'll discuss it at our next board meeting." Jezabelle's brusque tone was not lost on her friends.

Miranda moved forward to cover for Jezabelle's disapproval. "Why, that's quite a nice job you did here. Just a few pieces left. Why don't you go and ask your mother if she has another difficult puzzle.

We'll finish this one and take a picture." She took Junior's arm, indicating he should stand, and ushered him out the door.

"Well, that was tactful," Phoebe accused, glaring at Miranda indicating her disapproval of the way Miranda and Jezabelle had handled Junior.

Mr. Warbler was already examining the pictures on the wall and the memorabilia in the cases. He shook his head. "The items in these cases belonged to the Brilliant Brothers, but there's no mention of their wives or their families. All the brothers are listed on things such as this pipe; it belonged to Barnabas Brilliant.

The others joined him looking in the cases and on the walls. "Well Braxton was quite the artist. He painted this portrait. But it doesn't say who it is." Jezabelle leaned in close to the portrait to see if she was missing something.

"Here's a report card for Barton. It looks like he hit it off the charts in school." Phoebe pointed to a small card in a glass case.

"Here's a new puzzle for all of you! Junior said to tell you he had to go to work but he'd check with you later to see if he's been accepted into the Penderghast Puzzle Protectors. What are you all doing?" Marion entered the room setting the puzzle on the table.

"Marion, we were wondering if there was a book or something that had the history of the Brilliant Brothers here. We were curious about their family. All the history in the cases is about the seven brothers but not a word about their children or their wives." Jezabelle continued scouring the cases waiting for Marion's answer.

"There's a book but we keep it under lock and key since it's the only recorded history of the

Brilliant Brothers and their founding of this community. Apparently they weren't big into documenting what they were doing. They just built it, the same with their families. We have no pictures of their wives or their children. Let me get the book. We keep it in the safe and bring it out when someone wants to see it." Marion left the room to find the book.

Phoebe sat down at the table and the others joined her. Mr. Warbler finished the last few pieces of the puzzle Junior had been working on. Miranda took a picture of the puzzle so they'd have evidence that the Penderghast Puzzle Protectors was preserving the art of putting together puzzles when an agitated Marion entered the room.

"It's gone! It's gone! I unlocked the safe and it's gone. Call the police!"

"Are you sure you locked it away last time someone looked at it?" Mr. Warbler asked.

Miranda took Marion's arm and led her to a chair while Jezabelle got a glass of water from the water fountain using one of the paper cups they kept on hand.

"That's just it! I can't remember the last time someone asked for it. We have a special safe for it and it's the only thing kept in that safe. No one's asked for that book in years as far as I'm aware of." Marion began wringing her hands. "Oh, dear! Oh dear! I'll lose my job on this one. I have no idea how long it's been gone and who would have a key. We only have one key and we keep it locked up in the other safe. Only the librarians know the combination. The book could have been gone for years. It's the only record we have, oh dear, oh dear."

"Calm down, I'll call HH and the police will get to the bottom of this." Jezabelle picked up her cell phone and walked into the main part of the library to call Hank.

The others stayed behind to calm Marion. "Marion, do you recall if that book said anything about the Mudd farm?" Miranda asked, trying to distract Marion from the theft.

Marion looked up at Miranda who was standing over her, rubbing her shoulders to calm her down. "Mudd farm? I've never heard of it. But I must admit, I've never read the book. I'm not a big history fan and I'm not originally from Brilliant. Remember, Junior and I have only been here about five years. I moved here to take this job."

"The police are on their way," Jezabelle announced returning to the room. "Hank wasn't happy when he heard we were here."

"But we didn't have anything to do with this," Phoebe protested. "All we did was ask for a book."

Lizzy rushed into the room. "Come on all, we've got to go! I've made an appointment for us in one hour and we need to go home and pick up my drawings first." She stopped, noticing Marion's light sobs echoing throughout the room. "What happened?"

"It appears the book with the history of the Brilliant Brothers has disappeared," Mr. Warbler informed Lizzy.

Lizzy sat down. "Oh, okay, well, we have a few minutes we can help you look for it."

Marion's sobs reached decibel level. Lizzy looked at Jezabelle. "Something I said?"

Jezabelle sighed. "No, but it appears the book has been stolen out of a locked safe that hasn't been opened in years. Hank and his deputies are on their way over."

"And you know what that means," Phoebe reminded Lizzy.

Lizzy frowned. "No, what does that mean?"

"It means we're here at the scene again!" Phoebe said emphatically. "We will again get hauled over to the police station for questioning."

Lizzy stood up, "We can't—we have an appointment. Let's go before the police get here!"

"Isn't that leaving the scene of the crime?" Mr. Warbler questioned.

Jezabelle stood up. "No, Lizzy is right. We didn't discover the crime, Marion did."

"And, we weren't here when the crime was committed because we don't know when it happened," Phoebe agreed.

"Right, all you did was ask about the book so we can leave and it's not as if they don't know where to find us," Lizzy reminded them.

Jezabelle turned to Marion. "I'm sorry, Marion, but we have to leave you. We have an appointment. We'll call Junior to come and be with you and if you need someone to bail you out, call us and when we're done with our appointment, we'll arrange bail."

"But... but, you can't just leave me," Marion protested through her tears.

"Marion, this is bigger than all of us. Trust us when we tell you we won't leave you out to dry, but this appointment might solve Fred Rally's murder, Hick's attack, and be connected to whoever stole the book. You can handle this; you're strong!" Miranda took Marion by her shoulders. "Look me in the eye and repeat after me—I am strong!"

Marion meekly looked Miranda in her eyes and with a sniff repeated the words, "I am strong. I am strong." She lifted her shoulders and sat up straight giving a final sniff. "I can do this."

"I hear the sirens; we better skedaddle," Mr. Warbler advised the group. "We need to go out the back door."

The group moved to the back door, but not before they all turned while standing in the hole in the wall door and said as a group to Marion, "You are strong!"

CHAPTER FORTY-ONE

After leaving the library, the Penderghast Puzzle Protectors—minus Rock Stone—met at Miranda's to plan their strategy. They could see across the street so they'd know when Fleck Flaherty arrived at Annabelle's house.

"Explain to me what we're doing again and why we have to go to Annabelle's house?" Mr. Warbler questioned the group while nervously wringing his hands.

"Warbler, we discussed this. What's the matter with you? We need to check out Annabelle's floor and see if we can see what looks like a rainbow and a bar on the floor all intertwined with the letter *D*. We might have just been seeing scratches on that old photo at The BeDazzle." Phoebe grabbed Warbler's hands to stop him from wringing them.

Miranda raised her eyebrows at Warbler; Jezabelle had a thoughtful look on her face but kept quiet.

Lizzy was doodling on a piece of paper. "Wow, the clues just keep getting stranger and stranger. Do you suppose whoever stole that book is the same one who's been causing all this other ruckus with your neighborhood?"

"I'd guess that the book was stolen first and there was information in it that led the thief to think there was a puzzle here and made him want to solve it," Miranda stated.

"But if it's just a puzzle for fun—which is what the Brilliant brothers did—why go to such extremes to solve it?" Mr. Warbler rubbed his chin, a thoughtful look on his face.

Miranda was paging through the puzzle book she'd had found. "We haven't looked at this book too much because we were more interested in solving our puzzle after finding out that the Brilliant brothers were puzzle makers. But look! In this book of puzzles, all the puzzles lead to a treasure! Maybe there *is* an actual treasure at the end of the puzzle. The puzzles in our floors and the map are the clues!"

"That lead us to the treasure. This is a treasure hunt!" Jezabelle exclaimed. "We're looking for hidden treasure!"

Jezabelle's phone rang as they saw Fleck Flaherty drive up and park in Annabelle's driveway. "Yup... nope... can't... later... no more... that's it." Jezabelle hung up her phone. "That was Hank; we're off the hook since we were only asking about the book. Apparently, if we hadn't asked to see that book, it might have been a long time before the library even noticed it was missing. Let's go house hunting!" she said, leading the way across the street to Annabelle's and Fleck.

Mr. Warbler stopped in the middle of the street and turned to Jezabelle. "What about Marion?"

"Keep walking, Warbler; I can walk and talk at the same time," Jezabelle reminded him. "There's going to be a town council meeting to see if they want to keep her on as librarian. Hank urged us all to attend to vouch for her. But apparently the town council doesn't want to meet on the matter until the crime is solved, so they know what decision they should make."

"Of course, we'll stick up for her," Warbler stated. "Anyone who likes puzzles is top-notch in my book."

"Lizzy, I see you brought most of the Penderghast Puzzle Protectors," Fleck commented as he met the group by the curb in front of Annabelle's house. "You aren't going to convert this house into a puzzle, are you?" Fleck Flaherty winked at Lizzy.

Lizzy took Fleck's arm as they walked toward Annabelle's house. "No... my sister isn't a puzzle fan, but she certainly likes old architecture."

Fleck unlocked the door and ushered the group into the house. "As you can see, it's been very well kept. Annabelle had a deep reverence for history. She left the house mainly as it was built except for the addition of more modern amenities. We believe Baxter Brilliant lived in this house."

"Did he have any family?" Lizzy asked innocently, trying to see if Fleck had any information he hadn't shared.

"Yes, I believe he had a wife and children," Fleck answered, "but I can't tell you how many or their names. The only reason I suspect that is because there are notches and heights carved in the woodwork but we have no documentation except for what Baxter recorded. It's as if the families existed at that time, but it wasn't documented anywhere how many children or their names. At least that we can find."

"Did you know that Brilliant was very small in the beginning when the houses were built?" Miranda informed the realtor. Only the brothers, their wives, and their wives' families lived in Brilliant. I was able to find that much out on the

Internet. We think when they married, they moved their in-laws into town too."

"I wish I'd paid more attention to that plat map that was stolen," Fleck commented. "I think it had the names of the original farms and who owned them. We have documentation for everything after the Brilliant brothers and their families died or disappeared. Being a realtor, I've done some research on this. It appears they all just vanished one night and left the houses and the farms empty. It became almost a ghost town for a year until people from other communities and the government realized they weren't coming back. So others settled in their houses. The memorabilia in the Brilliant Brothers' Room are those things that were left by the brothers and their families."

The group stared at Fleck. "How did you find all this out?" Jezabelle asked. "And why didn't we know this? I've lived in Brilliant a long time."

"I'm kind of a history buff and Marion seemed to know these things. I asked a lot of questions when I was in the library one day."

"She must have gotten that from the book that's missing," Phoebe surmised. "I guess we didn't ask the right questions. Let's look at the house."

Walking into the living room, Jezabelle noticed the floor was in pristine shape. "How did the floor get repaired so quickly? It looks almost identical to the original floor except for the missing carvings."

"Can't have a floor with plywood or a hole in it if I'm going to sell this place for Annabelle's family," Fleck answered.

The group wandered around the house, making comments about Lizzy's sister, not wanting Fleck to notice as they wandered around that they were actually examining the carving around the edge of the floor that was in the shape of a *D*, a rainbow shape on one side, and a bar on the other.

"We need to see the basement," Lizzy announced. "After all, I have to make sure this house has a strong foundation so my sister doesn't have a house topple on her. I'd feel guilty if she was smashed in the middle of the night. It would be all my fault."

Fleck laughed and took Lizzy's arm. "This is an old house and no one ever bothered to put an inside stairway to the basement. We have to go outside to get into the basement." He led the way and the others followed.

Jezabelle stopped outside the back door. "We need to see the garage too. I never noticed before but it looks like a tiny cottage or gatehouse. It's not built like the rest of our garages."

Mr. Warbler knocked into Jezabelle. "Oh, sorry, Jezabelle, I must have tripped. Let's look at the basement." Mr. Warbler grabbed Jezabelle and moved her to the side of the house by the basement door.

Jezabelle moved her arm out of Warbler's grasp. "Okay, alright."

Miranda joined them, glaring at Warbler. Seeing Miranda's glare, he lowered his eyes.

"The gatehouse and garage have been sold," said Fleck. "Annabelle's family decided to divide up the large yard and they sold it before I became their realtor. It was a private sale. There's a private drive in the back that those owners use so you wouldn't see them. Let's check out this basement." Fleck reached down and opened the cellar door into the basement. "I'll go first and flick on the lights."

The stone steps leading to the basement were deep. The women held onto the side so they wouldn't fall. Warbler followed, holding onto both sides of the stone walls as his large body almost touched both sides.

Lizzy nodded her head. "Not a bad basement. Old-fashioned but someone seems to have done some work here to make it usable."

A rustling in the corner of the basement broke into her musings. Everyone but Fleck jumped back at the sound.

"It's a mouse!" Phoebe screamed.

"Or a squirrel. It's making too much noise for a mouse, and I know squirrels," Mr. Warbler stated.

Jezabelle peered into the corner and laughed. "No, it's Mr. Shifty and Mrs. Mysterious hiding underneath that shelf and they're batting at something that's crumpled up. She reached down and grabbed the crumpled-up paper. "How did you get in here? It's time you came home." She picked up Mr. Shifty and handed him to Lizzy. Reaching down, she picked up Mrs. Mysterious and handed her to Miranda.

Fleck was staring at a window in the corner of the basement. "Ah, I see, this window must not have been latched and they pushed it open." He walked over, closed it tight, and latched it.

"What's on the paper, Jezabelle? The floor's pretty clean; it must have been stuck underneath the shelf." Phoebe walked over to take the paper out of Jezabelle's hands.

Jezabelle quickly glanced at the paper and stuck it in her pocket. "Looks like an old grocery list. I'll toss it when I get home. Don't want to leave any trash around for prospective buyers." She moved to the stairs and continued up the steps.

Once they were all outside, Fleck asked, "So Lizzy, what do you think? Would your sister like this house?"

Lizzy nodded her head. "It has its possibilities. I'll stop in your office tomorrow after I talk to her and, if she's agreeable, I'll make an offer."

Fleck held out his hand to Lizzy. "Great! I'll see you tomorrow. Since you all live nearby, I'll be on my way."

The group watched as Fleck walked down the driveway, got into his car, and drove away.

Jezabelle turned to Lizzy. "Your sister's going to make an offer? Wasn't that kind of cruel to get the man's hopes up about a sale? When are you going to tell him you don't have a sister?"

Lizzy smiled as she grabbed Jezabelle's arm to lead her down the driveway. "Maybe never."

CHAPTER FORTY-TWO

Jezabelle hurried down the street to her house, pulling Lizzy with her. The others followed trying to keep up the pace.

"Jezabelle, tell us what the paper says!" Phoebe hollered trying to match Jezabelle's pace.

"I will, when we're in the house." She reached her porch steps and quickly unlocked her door. Only then did she turn, let loose of Lizzy, and wait for the others to catch up. She held the door for them to enter.

Miranda and Phoebe set the cats down on the floor. "Have you ever tried hurrying while carrying two wiggly fur balls?" Miranda asked.

"What's the hurry?" Mr. Warbler was breathing hard after the fast dash down the street.

"Jezabelle likes to make a fast getaway," Lizzy teased.

"The note says, *May you have all the happiness and luck that life can hold. And at the end of your rainbows may you find a pot of gold.*"

Miranda wrinkled her nose in thought. "That's not a bible verse but an old Irish blessing."

Jezabelle nodded. "They changed the clues."

"Or maybe... the clues actually didn't have anything to do with the bible; they just used them for clues because they fit what they wanted to lead people to," Lizzy suggested.

"It's gold! We're looking for gold!" Phoebe shouted, excitedly doing an Irish jig around the room.

"Where's the rainbow?" Warbler asked, lifting his hands and dropping them down in defeat.

"We'll find it," Jezabelle assured him.

"Now we know the bar intertwined in the *D* is a gold bar," Miranda stated. "Or at least we think so."

"What do we do next?" Warbler asked.

Jezabelle entered her kitchen and came out with a bottle of wine.

"It's only three o'clock!" Phoebe's horrified look accompanied her statement. "We can't drink this early in the afternoon."

"We can." Lizzy took the bottle out of Jezabelle's hands. She moved to the built-in china cabinet in the dining room and, taking out glasses, poured each one a drink.

"We are now entering our final strategy session." Jezabelle lifted her glass to toast the others. "Hopefully, by this time tomorrow we'll have some answers, but first we have to ask some questions."

The others raised their glasses.

"Miranda, would you write down the questions in an orderly manner?" Jezabelle asked.

"I guess we'd better sit down for this. This could take a long time," Phoebe surmised.

"What about Rock? Shouldn't he be here?" Mr. Warbler asked.

"I'll fill him in when he gets home tonight and see what he thinks, although that could take a while. Maybe a glass of wine would make him talk faster. I might have to try that," Jezabelle answered.

"What are the questions?" Miranda sat poised with her pen.

"Why was Hick digging up the grave?" Phoebe threw out the question.

"Did he find anything in the grave and is that why someone tried to kill him?" Lizzy added.

"Is the Hickory we know and trust part of this?" Mr. Warbler shook his head not wanting to even entertain that possibility.

"Is there anything in the other graves?" Jezabelle threw the question to Miranda.

"Where is the book? Is that what we need to solve the puzzle?" Miranda wrote the question down as she spoke.

"Is the bar a *gold* bar and where do we look for it?" Phoebe was still dreaming of the gold.

"And why would the Brilliant brothers hide a gold bar and why did they disappear?" Lizzy said.

"Why was Fred Rally killed? How does he tie into this or was he just an innocent bystander falling into a bad situation?" Jezabelle asked.

Mr. Warbler choked on his wine. "Falling— that's a good one Jezabelle." He chuckled.

The others laughed at Jezabelle's words.

Jezabelle ignored them, still deep in thought. "We might also want to ask ourselves what was on the paper they found on my floor and Warbler's floor and why does Rock not have a letter of the alphabet on his floor."

"Well, we just asked the questions," Miranda pointed out. "The problem is we have no answers. Where do we go from here?" She wrote a big question mark over the entire paper.

Jezabelle stood up. "I'm going to bake. I always think better when I'm baking. Tomorrow, bright and early, we're going to visit Hick in the hospital and ask him some of those questions, and then we will revisit the scene of the crime. I'll call HH and see if they've dug up the other graves yet and we'll meet tomorrow morning. I'll also see if Rock wants to take the day off and come with us. He might have some valuable insight since he's had some time and distance from the case."

Lizzy's eyes grew wide at the mention of calling HH. "Do you think it's a good idea to call Hank? Then he'll know the Penderghast Puzzle Protectors are still solving puzzles and he'll find a way to stop us."

Jezabelle had a sly look on her face. "I'll ply him with a chocolate peanut butter cup cheesecake, and he won't know what he told me. I'll invite him to stop by at around seven for dessert."

Miranda stood up, pen still in hand, still doodling on her tablet. "We'll meet at my house. I'll see if I can borrow a van from a friend and then we all can fit into the same vehicle." She gave a pointed look to Warbler, but the others—lost in thought—didn't notice.

"I'm a fan of a van!" Jezabelle laughed as she ushered them out the door.

CHAPTER FORTY-THREE

"Did you talk to Hank Hardy last night?" Miranda greeted Jezabelle the next day, opening the door to let her in.

"Yup, plied him with cheesecake, sent him out the door at eight. All I found out was since there was no body in the grave they saw no reason to dig up the others. Apparently, Hick was digging up the graves for someone from out of town who said they were the new owners and they wanted the bodies relocated to the Brilliant Cemetery."

The old-fashioned doorbell rang, interrupting Jezabelle's story. Miranda motioned for Lizzy, Mr. Warbler, and Phoebe to come in and join them. Nodding to Jezabelle, she said, "Go on."

"I told Hank it didn't make sense because no one knew the cemetery was there. It wasn't even on the original plat map that you found, Miranda."

"So did Hick find anything in the grave?" Lizzy asked.

"Hank wouldn't tell me; said it was part of the investigation and we weren't part of the investigation." Jezabelle's miffed tone matched her face.

"Humph." Phoebe rolled her eyes. "I guess cheesecake wouldn't loosen his lips." She blew on her nails. "You should have let me work my feminine wiles on him."

A pounding on the door interrupted Jezabelle. "It's... time... to go. Although... I don't... know...

where… we're… going." Rock Stone paused at the open door before turning around and moving to the van in the driveway.

"I take it he's driving?" Mr. Warbler followed Rock to the van.

"Nice van, where did you get it, Miranda?" Phoebe asked.

They heard a thump from the side passenger door. Mr. Warbler fell out of the van.

Rock Stone got back out of the van to help the large man get up and back into the van. "Don't… forget to… fasten… your seatbelt. We… don't… want to lose… you… on a… corner." Getting back in the van, he turned and yelled to Jezabelle who was tucked into the corner of the last seat in the van. "Where… are we… going?"

"To the hospital. We need to talk to Hick," Jezabelle instructed.

On the way to the hospital, the conversation turned to their plan. "I think after we interview Hick, we should go back to the crime scene, "Lizzy suggested.

"Which one?" Phoebe asked.

"The farm," Lizzy answered. I think we should check out the gravesite again and the rest of the property.

"There's nothing left there but the barn and the burned-down house," Phoebe reminded her.

"Yes, but if there were supposed to be bodies, we need to ask Hick how he was supposed to get them out through all that brush." Lizzy presented the dilemma to the group.

"You're right, Lizzy, why didn't we think of that before?" Jezabelle agreed.

"We... are... here! Be... careful... getting... out. There are... cans of... paint... sitting... on the... car floor. They... might... spill!" Rock cautioned.

Being careful not to spill the paint cans, the group exited the van.

"Who did you borrow this van from anyway, Miranda? Are they a painter?" Phoebe pushed aside a can so it wouldn't fall out the door.

Mr. Warbler yowled, "Oww!"

"Warbler, what's the matter with you?" Lizzy moved to his side.

"Got stung by a bee! I think it's okay now." He rubbed his arm.

Lizzy picked up his arm and gave it a keen look. "Can't see anything." She leaned down and gave it a quick kiss. "There—it will be better."

Jezabelle couldn't believe what she saw Lizzy do so she walked into the hospital before her tongue got the better of her and she chided her best friend.

"Hickory Rafferty, please," she said to the receptionist. The receptionist pointed to the room across from her desk. Jezabelle led the group into Hickory's room.

"Oh, Jezabelle, you're a glimmer of hope and so beautiful today!" Hick's eyes twinkled at seeing Jezabelle.

"Well, youngster, you need to get out of here. I miss my morning flirting practice." Jezabelle patted his hand.

Miranda stepped forward. "Mr. Rafferty, I don't know if you've heard, but we're the Penderghast Puzzle Protectors and we're trying to solve the puzzle of some missing pieces of floor, and we think your attack had something to do with it. What can you tell us?" She took out her pen and paper.

"Is that the neighbor of yours I've never seen—the author?" Hickory asked Jezabelle.

Jezabelle nodded.

"She's a looker, Jezabelle, you need to talk her into coming out to our flirting practice." Hick winked at Miranda.

Miranda cleared her throat. "Yes, well, can you answer the question?"

Phoebe pushed Miranda back and stepped forward. "What's with all this business-like tone?" She turned to Hick. "Spill it! What do you know?"

"I know I'm not supposed to talk to you, order of Hank Hardy, Chief of Police."

Rock Stone stepped forward. "I'll... take... care of... this." He leaned forward and whispered something in Hick's ear.

Hick turned red, sputtered a little, and began to talk. "I got a phone call, and the person said they heard I dug graves. They said that they needed one grave dug on the old Darnel property. They were going to relocate it. I was to dig up the grave and leave the casket in the grave. Someone would come by later in the afternoon to move it; although once I found the site, I didn't see how they were going to move the casket. I dug and dug but didn't uncover a casket, but a metal box. It wasn't locked. I started to open the box and that's all I remember."

"You don't know what was in the box?" Jezabelle questioned.

"I'm not sure—my memory's still foggy, but I thought I got a glimpse of an old metal key. Sorry that's all I remember."

"Hick, are you sure you're not in on this?" Mr. Warbler gave him a stern look.

"Have you seen my head? I'm giving up grave digging and sticking to garbage," Hick told the group.

"If you think of anything else, let us know," Miranda told him. She gave him her card.

Hick glanced at the card. "Now I can flirt over the phone. You're an author; maybe I'll study your writings."

Miranda blushed and rushed from the room. The others laughed and Jezabelle winked at Hick as she followed the others out of the room.

CHAPTER FORTY-FOUR

"Maybe... we... should... not stop. There... seem... to be a... few... police cars... here," Rock Stone informed the group as he pulled the van into the driveway of the old Darnel farm that they now knew was the old Mudd farm.

Jezabelle peered through the front windshield from the front seat of the van. "Something's going on. We got here just in time."

"That's Hank's car. He's going to tell us to leave," Phoebe pointed out.

"They must be back by the cemetery. I don't see anyone here." Mr. Warbler climbed out of the van.

Rock Stone got out, walked over to the burned down house, and silently waited to see what the others wanted to do.

Jezabelle opened her van door and hopped out. "Let's go!" She sprinted towards the path behind the barn before anyone could stop her.

"She can sure move fast for an old lady," Phoebe commented before following Jezabelle.

Jezabelle didn't waste any time getting to the hidden cemetery, the path having been trampled so much lately that there wasn't much brush to push out of the way. When she arrived, she saw Hank and Hanna talking by another open grave. Stick and Jeb were talking to Snoop Steckle by the third open grave while Snoop was taking pictures.

"You allowed Snoop out here and you didn't call us to see you dig up these graves?" Jezabelle chastised Hank. "You didn't tell me this last night."

A wide grin spread across Hank Hardy's face. "I was too busy enjoying the cheesecake, and you only asked if we'd dug up the graves *yet,* so technically I was telling you the truth. You asked the wrong question."

Lizzy stopped Jezabelle from saying something she might regret and getting herself arrested. "Hank, what did you find?"

Hank shook his head. "Nothing—empty graves."

Rock, Phoebe, and Mr. Warbler joined the deputies and Snoop Steckle as they were speculating on why the graves were empty.

"That makes no sense. Hick said he found a box," Jezabelle reminded him.

"Nope. No boxes and no bodies in these graves. The twenty-four dollar question is—why would the Brilliant brothers want us to think there were graves here?" Hank asked, thinking aloud.

"I got it! I got it! I got the scoop!" Snoop Steckle snickered in glee. He snapped a picture of the entire group. "I can see the headline now: Brilliant Police Department and the Penderghast Puzzle Protectors puzzled by lack of evidence. Who will solve the puzzle—the puzzled police or the puzzled puzzlers?" Snoop quickly took off down the path but not before he'd placed a kiss on Hanna's cheek in passing.

Hank gave Hanna a suspicious look. "What was that?"

Jezabelle punched Hank lightly in the arm. "That's what happens when you let the media mongrels in on the scene of a crime."

Hank took Jezabelle's arm as he turned to his deputies. "Fill in the graves, we're done here."

He began to walk toward the path, taking Jezabelle with him. "I'll explain as we all go back to our cars and leave our deputies to their task."

Rock Stone took one last look in the grave and indicated to the others they should follow Hank and Jezabelle. They took his lead but not before each of them peered into the empty graves, shaking their heads in confusion.

"We thought we might get some kind of lead if we let our citizens in on what is happening," Hank explained. "Maybe someone knows something they don't know they know."

Hank's cell phone rang just as they reached their cars. "Hardy here—I'll be right there." Hank redialed his phone. "Hanna, you and Jeb get your cars and meet me at the fire station. Leave Stick behind and have him call Fuchsia and see if one of their deputies can come and help him finish up with those graves. We don't want anyone besides the police on that site. I'll explain later." Hank ended his call. "Sorry, folks; I have to go and I expect you will leave too."

"You... are... going... to the... fire station?" Rock Stone asked.

Hank nodded. "You must be working the night shift since you're here, Stone. Have Jezzy send some cheesecake with you; it'll help you get through." Turning to Jezabelle and her friends, he added, "Jezzy, you and your friends go home. No more snooping and I'd suggest you stay there until you hear from me." He gave her a stern look. "There's been another development and I want to make sure you're all safe." Hank got in his car and

drove away before any of them could ask any
questions.

CHAPTER FORTY-FIVE

The Penderghast Puzzle Protectors congregated in Miranda's house, except for Rock Stone who said he needed to get some sleep before working the night shift.

"Did we ever ask Rock where he worked?" Phoebe asked, looking out the window watching Rock walk across the street to his house.

"Did you ever ask him who the woman is that visited him the night I stayed with you, Jezabelle?" Lizzy walked to the window to watch with Phoebe. "He's awfully cute—must be about thirty-five. I wonder why he's keeping his girlfriend a secret."

Phoebe jumped on the word *girlfriend*. "He's around thirty-five? I thought he might be younger that's why I never showed any interest. I didn't want to be accused of being a cougar but... I'm only a few years older."

"So much for solving the crime today; we didn't learn much of anything," Mr. Warbler reminded them.

"We did if we're going to believe Hick. We learned there was a box with a key in one grave, the grave that has the name *Charity* on it. We learned the other graves are empty."

Miranda had been studying her notes. "We have the puzzle solved as far as the cemetery goes."

"We must be missing something, don't you think, Jezabelle?" noticing Jezabelle's faraway look.

Jezabelle stood up and paced back and forth for a few seconds. "Do you suppose the fire at the old Mudd house has anything to do with the puzzle? After all, the clues led us to the old Mudd farm. We don't know why the Mudd farm, but we have to surmise that possibly the Mudds were related to one of the wives of one of the brothers."

Mr. Warbler nodded in agreement. "You might be right. They were puzzle masters and, according to what we've learned, the entire town was built with a puzzle in mind including our houses, so why not carry that to the Mudd house? It would be perfect."

"But why burn down the house?" Phoebe asked.

"Our murderer found a clue to where the treasure is and didn't want anyone else to find it?" Mr. Warbler guessed.

Jezabelle's cell phone broke into their musings. "I don't recognize this number." She answered the phone anyway not wanting to miss winning another cruise. The telemarketers were always calling her about cruises and she was keeping count of how many she'd won. She figured she'd be able to cruise for the rest of her life on all the cruises she'd supposedly won. "Where is my cruise going this time?"

Miranda shook her head and raised her eyes before returning to her notes. The others indicated to Jezabelle she should hang up.

Jezabelle put her hand out to still their whispering. "I see. We'll be right down. Thank you, Marion. I'm sorry to hear that though. Yes, we'll keep you posted if we hear more."

"What? What?" Phoebe anxiously peered into Jezabelle's face.

"George Grifter is dead. They found him at the fire station. And—they found the missing book from the library in his locker at the station. Marion has it now. HH brought it back to her a few minutes ago."

"What! George dead? How? Heart Attack?" Lizzy gasped in shock.

"According to Marion, they aren't sure yet. It looks like he could've had a heart attack but he was there by himself at the time. They won't know until an autopsy is done," Jezabelle explained. "Marion said we could come down and take a look at the book."

"I don't believe it!" Mr. Warbler began pacing. "If he had the book, then he must have been behind the murder of Fred and our floornapping. You mean he helped rescue me when all along he was the one that caused my fall?"

"We need to look at that book! I'm sure Hank looked at it and must have decided they didn't need it for anything or they wouldn't have given it back to Marion." Jezabelle put in her two cents' worth.

Miranda made a mark on her page of notes. "Now we have the book, the puzzle pieces, the place the pieces lead us to, but we don't know where the rainbow and the gold are."

"And if George knew, he's not telling. Dead men don't talk," Phoebe added.

Lizzy laughed. "You've been watching too many television shows, Phoebe."

Miranda stood up looking at her notes. "Here's what doesn't add up. One: What was Fred Rally doing in Annabelle's house? I know he told me he lived in an old house but wouldn't we have known if he was living in Annabelle's house so why was he there? It cost him his life. Two: Did George Grifter start the fire at the old Mudd place after reading the book and finding a clue? And then call the fire department to put out a fire?"

Jezabelle continued, "Three: Who called the police about my floor? We forgot about that. Who knew the floornappers were at my house?"

"And how does it all tie together? Friends, we have our work cut out for us." Miranda put down her notepad. "We'd better get going before the book gets stolen again. The van is still in the driveway. I wonder if Rock's friend would mind if we used it? He forgot to return it. Do you think the key is still in the van?" She looked pointedly at Mr. Warbler.

Flustered, Warbler headed toward the door so he could avoid her eyes. "Well, that would be kind of stupid, but let's check. After all, they're stealing floors, not cars." Turning around at the door, he said to the others, "Well, are you coming? I'll drive!"

CHAPTER FORTY-SIX

Marion was waiting for the Penderghast Puzzle Protectors when they arrived at the library. She ushered them through the Hole in the Wall into the Brilliant Brothers' Memorial Room. The *book* was sitting on the table.

Jezabelle was the first to reach the book. She picked it up and began to page through its fragile old pages.

"Jezabelle, I want to see the book," Phoebe pleaded.

Lizzy, who'd driven her own car down to the library so she wouldn't have to go back to the Penderghast neighborhood, entered the room and, hearing Phoebe, scolded, "Let the woman have time to contemplate what she's looking at."

Jezabelle held up her hand for them all to be silent. "This book documents the building of the library, the bank, the saloon, and a few other buildings, along with our houses. It also has the floor plans for our houses along with detailed drawings of our floors."

Still paging through the book, Jezabelle sat down at the table to silently read a few more pages before continuing, "There's apparently no documentation on anything about a puzzle or about the families. It does list all the Brilliant brothers' names."

Lizzy took the book from Jezabelle and laughed at what she saw. "Their mother liked *B*s. Listen to their names: Braxton, Barton, Bennet, Bertrand, Benedict, Broderick, Bartholomew, and Barnabas."

Mr. Warbler piped up, "Well, she certainly liked the Bs—do you suppose she liked the birds too?"

"And the flowers and the trees?" Lizzy laughed.

Warbler moved toward Lizzy. "And the moon up above?"

Lizzy answered, "And this thing called love."

Jezabelle watched her two friends through suspicious eyes before turning to Marion. "Didn't you tell someone that the first three Brilliant brothers were married and the women's names were Faith, Hope, and Charity. And if I remember right, I was told that there was no mention of their children's names or wives' names anywhere and they just snuck out of town leaving everything behind and it became a ghost town for a year or two? There must have been other people living here, too, if they had all these buildings. How did you know that? You told us you never read this book and this book has no information about any of that."

"Well, uh... if I did."

"You did," Lizzy reminded her.

"Well, uh, I didn't want to appear that I, the head librarian, didn't know anything about the history of Brilliant so I just repeated some of the gossip I'd heard when I moved to Brilliant and the rest I made up. And... I didn't read that book. History bores me."

"You're a librarian and history bores you?" Phoebe was about to say more when Hank Hardy made his appearance at the Hole in the Wall.

"I see most of you are here. I thought I told you to stay home. It appears that George Grifter stole the book and whether he's the one who floornapped your floors, hurt Hick, and set the old Mudd house on fire is still to be determined. Although from the looks of that book, I don't know why he would've had the idea to heist your floors and the carved wall in this room because there's nothing in that book that mentions a reason for it."

"We think the puzzles lead to gold," Phoebe offered up the tidbit to Hank to impress him as she moved closer so she could touch his arm. "Would you like to help us investigate?" she purred.

Jezabelle grabbed Phoebe's arm and yanked her away from Hank while whispering in her ear, "Why did you tell him that? It was our little secret."

"Something you're not telling me, Jezzy?" Hank met Jezabelle's eyes.

Jezabelle averted her eyes. "Have you ever heard of anything so ridiculous? If there were gold here, you'd know it, wouldn't you?"

"Did Grifter have a heart attack?" Miranda who'd been silent, spoke up. "Or do you think it was murder?"

All eyes turned to Hank. Hank reached over and took the book from Lizzy who still had it in her hands. "Only the body knows for sure, and it's over at the morgue for the autopsy now." He handed the book to Marion. "Better lock this up tight, although I think we'll have no more trouble."

"Does that mean we can work on solving the rest of the puzzle in safety?" Jezabelle threw out the question even though she knew the answer.

"No! Leave the puzzle solving to the police! We have too many loose ends to tie up. You people just stick to putting cardboard puzzles together."

Jezabelle sniffed. "Well, I thought I'd ask. Warbler, take us home. I've got some baking I want to do. Maybe I'll send a cheesecake to work with

Rock tonight. Maybe I can catch him before he leaves and fill him in."

"I'll just lock this back up then," said Marion. "If you all want to see it again, just let me know. Junior said to ask if I saw you if you'd decided if he could join your group. Have you made a decision?"

The Penderghast Puzzle Protectors quickly shuffled out of the library, Phoebe taking Hanks' arm and pulling him out the door with her, leaving Jezabelle to answer Marion. "You know, when we decide, we'll stop by and tell him in person. Where does he live?" Jezabelle avoided giving Marion an answer.

"He's neither here nor there right now. You can tell me when you decide and I'll make sure he gets the message."

Jezabelle wrinkled her nose. "Here not there? Well, if he's not here he must be there. Where is there?"

Marion jumped. "Speaking of there, I'm not supposed to be here; I'm supposed to be there." Marion quickly exited the room toward the back of the library.

Jezabelle muttered to herself as she left the library, "Well, I'm here and I'm not there, but if I get in the van, I'll be somewhere."

CHAPTER FORTY-SEVEN

Jezabelle slipped back into her bedroom after sitting under the stars on her porch and having one last taste of wine. It had been a perfect evening. She had finished her baking and then she had a pleasant few hours of good company and wonderful conversation. She smiled remembering the turn of the conversation. With a sigh, she traversed down the steps to her kitchen to put the wine glasses in the sink.

Out of her kitchen window, she saw a car turn into Rock Stone's driveway. Quickly, she dashed the light in the kitchen so she could get a better look. She knew Rock wasn't home because earlier she was going to take a warm pie over to him to take to work when she saw him drive out of his driveway. Wiping her hands on a towel, she made a quick step into her back mudroom then watched the car through the glass door leading to the outside.

The car stopped, a woman got out, opened the garage door, and drove the car in. While the woman was in the garage, Jezabelle quietly opened her back door, stepped onto her back porch, and moved behind a bush close to the driveway. She watched as the woman walked from the garage to the back door, put a key in the lock, opened the door, and went into the house.

Jezabelle leaned against the tree. The woman now in Rock Stone's house looked a lot like Hanna Hardy through the darkness. Of course, she couldn't be sure, and… what would Hanna be doing at Rock Stone's at two in the morning? Jezabelle was sure Hanna was the same woman she and Lizzy had seen visiting Rock the other evening. Should she confront Hanna? Should she call Rock? Should she call Hank? Or should she leave it alone and see how it would play out?

Jezabelle decided for once in her life to leave it alone. Maybe the two were having a thing and Hanna didn't want Hank to know. Or maybe Hanna was feeding Rock's snake at two o'clock. After all, young folks did strange things. She'd wait for the right moment. Hanna wouldn't hurt anything and maybe she was undercover checking out Rock's house when he wasn't home. *But she sure seemed at home,* Jezabelle thought.

Back in the house, Jezabelle looked at the clock and saw that it was now two-thirty. The couch looked mighty soft. She sunk down onto the pillows, put her head back, and immediately fell asleep and began dreaming that someone was trying to stuff her into a book.

A loud crash woke Jezabelle. Opening her eyes, she took in her surroundings and saw the bright morning light coming through the window of her living room. She remembered—it was garbage day. Looking down, she saw she was still dressed from yesterday. Briskly sprinting out her front door, she retrieved the garbage can from the back of her house and dragged it to the end of her driveway.

"I knew you'd come running when you saw I was back!" Jezabelle turned to see Hick Rafferty back at his job.

"Hick, you're alive and you're here!" Jezabelle was so happy to see he was all right she jumped up and grabbed his tall frame around the neck and gave him a hug.

Hick twirled the tiny lady around in a circle. "I am and it's all because of you! If you hadn't found me, I'd be that tiny piece of ash scattered in your garden," he teased.

"Scatter ashes, good idea, I've thought of that, but hopefully you've got a lot of trash talking to do before that happens."

"Why, Jezabelle, I'd talk trash with you any day!" Hick laughed. "I do have something to tell you. I think I remember what I saw in that box. I think it was a large, rustic skeleton key and on the key was inscribed the word *charity*. I can't be sure. Maybe I dreamed it but I seem to think that was what I saw before my head exploded. I told Hank but he didn't seem too concerned."

"He's just throwing you off, doesn't want any of the good citizens of Brilliant to get involved. And he's right, Hick. If they knew you remembered what happened, they could come after you again!"

"Does anyone know who *they* is?" Hick asked.

"Well, speculation is that it was Grifter because he had the book, but I'm not so sure. It doesn't make sense. I've known him all his life and he was never the shady type, reckless maybe, but never shady."

Phoebe walked across the street joining the conversation. "Jezabelle," she said, looking Jezabelle up and down. "Didn't you wear those clothes yesterday?" She sniffed, indicating her disapproval.

Hick looked at the two women, wanting to leave before the verbal explosion. "I've got to go. I took on another garbage route to make up for my grave digging. I never want to see another grave that close again!" Hick hopped in his truck and started the engine.

Jezabelle and Phoebe watched the truck lumber down the road. Jezabelle's cell phone broke through the noise of the truck.

"Yup, they what? They are? We'll be right down." She plopped the phone in her pocket and turned to Phoebe. "Come on!"

"Where we going?"

"To the library."

"Has there been another theft?" Phoebe hurried down Jezabelle's driveway trying to keep up with Jezabelle.

"No—it seems Mrs. Mysterious and Mr. Shifty are at the library!"

Phoebe laughed. "Maybe they like to read." Phoebe got in the passenger side of Jezabelle's Smart Car. "This thing is tiny."

"It works," Jezabelle informed her as she backed out of the driveway almost hitting the garbage can she'd forgotten to put back in her garage.

"Can you park this thing better than you could your other cars? Maybe I should have driven," Phoebe suggested.

"Hang on!" Jezabelle warned as she came to the intersection of Strong and Roosevelt.

"Jezabelle, that car just missed you! What's the hurry?" Phoebe screamed.

"Marion doesn't like cats. Who knows what she'll do with them."

"Did you leave them at the library?" Phoebe asked.

"No, they tend to wander and they seem to find their way into basements, and they happened to be in basement of the library this morning when Marion opened up. Apparently, they growled at her when she went down to the basement to bring up some toilet paper for the women's restroom. She shooed them outside and now they're hiding in the bushes, and she says they're terrorizing the patrons. If I don't get there right away, she's calling Hank." Jezabelle pealed into the parking lot, at least as good a peal as she could with such a small car.

Marion was standing by the side of the library, pointing to the bushes. "They're going to ruin the bushes! I want them gone now!"

Phoebe whispered to Jezabelle, "What's wrong with her? I always thought she was this sweet older woman."

Jezabelle whispered back, keeping her eye on Marion, "Maybe the leopard is changing its spots."

"Huh." Phoebe's perplexed look was not lost on Marion.

"Phoebe, don't just stand there looking rich and pretty, help Jezabelle."

Jezabelle was already climbing under the bushes looking for the cats. "Mr. Shifty, get over here!" She made a grab at the cat but he ran for the library's open window that was hidden behind the bush. She made another grab and caught him just as he ducked under the open window and was on the inside sill. He grabbed something sitting on the sill and pulled it out with him. Now that Jezabelle had him, she wasn't going to take time to see what he had. "Phoebe, get over here and take him!" She handed the cat to Phoebe with whatever was in his mouth. "Warning, he might have a mouse in his mouth!"

Phoebe screamed but she held on to Mr. Shifty. "You can come out now, Jezabelle. Mrs. Mysterious is right here by my ankles. Apparently, she goes where Mr. Shifty goes." She paused for a minute.

"Jezabelle, Jezabelle, come out here right now! You won't believe what Mr. Shifty found."

Jezabelle crawled out from under the bushes picking prickly thorns out of her hair. "Marion, if you'd shut your basement window you wouldn't have cats!"

"She can't hear you; she went back inside the minute you went under the bush." Phoebe thrust something in Jezabelle's hands along with Mr. Shifty.

Jezabelle looked down. In one hand was a rustic key that was hanging on an old ribbon. Mr. Shifty, whom Jezabelle was holding in her arms, tried to grab the ribbon on the key. Jezabelle held on to the key tightly while reading what was etched on the barrel-like cylinder. It said *Charity*. She stuffed the key underneath Mr. Shifty as she held him in her arms. "We have to go home and call a meeting of the Penderghast Puzzle Protectors."

Phoebe leaned in and whispered, "Marion's watching from the window of the library."

"Pick up Mrs. Mysterious and act like you're happy to see her and then calmly walk to my car with me."

Phoebe did as she said. Jezabelle let out a loud belly laugh and tossed her head back.

"Laugh, Phoebe!"

Phoebe gave Jezabelle a skeptical look. "Why?"

"To look as if we are having a laugh at the cats so no one knows we may have found something," Jezabelle explained.

"We didn't find anything; Mr. Shifty did. The bigger question is why was it in the library? Do you suppose Marion knows something?"

"Get in the car, Phoebe; we have to get home." Jezabelle handed Mr. Shifty to Phoebe.

Phoebe took the cat and put him down on her lap next to Mrs. Mysterious. "Snuggle up you two, or should I say, buckle up. You've probably never driven with Mrs. Leadfoot."

CHAPTER FORTY-EIGHT

Instead of turning into her driveway, Jezabelle turned into Miranda Covington's driveway.

"We're going to Miranda's?" Phoebe inquired, still holding tightly onto the protesting felines that were in her lap.

"Yup, let the creatures out to run. Hopefully, they won't go back to the library. We need to show this key to Miranda and have a little huddle to come up with a plan."

Phoebe let loose of the cats when she opened her car door, and they were off her lap before she could say *scoot*. "Huddle?"

"Yes, as in football. We need to call the next play." Jezabelle launched her tiny body up the steps.

Phoebe followed, muttering, "Now we're playing football?"

Jezabelle was on the twentieth ring of the doorbell by the time Phoebe caught up with her. "She must be ensconced in writing and not hear the bell," Jezabelle guessed.

"Miranda's not home." Mr. Warbler waddled across his and Phoebe's yard.

"Where is she and how do you know she's not home?" Jezabelle asked, suspicious of Mr. Warbler's information.

"I saw her drive away this morning and, when she came back, she had Lizzy in the car. They parked the car in Miranda's garage and walked over to Rock Stone's."

Phoebe turned to Jezabelle. "Without us?" Phoebe turned back to Warbler. "Without you?"

"Oh, I could have joined them; they invited me but I was busy feeding my squirrels at the time. What ya got there in your hand?" Warbler asked seeing the key.

"A little souvenir from the basement of the library." Jezabelle handed the key to Warbler.

Warbler squinted and held the key close to his face. "It says *Charity*."

Phoebe, impatient by the banter, jumped up and down. "It's a clue! It's a clue!"

"We don't know that for sure, Phoebe; after all, it was at the library and not in our houses. We were going to show it to Miranda and call you and Lizzy," Jezabelle explained to Warbler.

"They think we missed something," said Warbler. "Rock doesn't have a design in his floor but it wasn't like the Brilliant brothers to leave out a piece of the puzzle in a house. Miranda called you and Phoebe, but you weren't answering your cell phones. She called Lizzy, but Lizzy didn't have a car—something about punctured tires, so Miranda picked her up and told me when I was in the yard." Warbler continued his explanation, "Apparently, she found another secret hiding place in her house, and it gave her an idea."

At the words, "cell phones turned off," Phoebe and Jezabelle reached in their pockets to check their phones. "I forgot mine at home," Phoebe deduced, finding an empty pocket.

Jezabelle looked at her phone. "I must have accidently turned mine off when I was hunting in the bushes."

Warbler looked at Jezabelle. "You were hunting? How could you hunt beautiful live creatures?"

Jezabelle rolled her eyes, switched on her cell phone, and walked away from the two on her way to Rock Stone's.

Warbler and Phoebe hurried to catch up.

The trio passed the front door and scurried around the house to the unlocked back door. "You hoo!" Phoebe called out, entering the house behind Jezabelle.

"We're up here!" Lizzy called down from the top of the steps leading up to the second floor. "We're looking for something we might have missed."

"We have Rock's permission." Miranda joined Lizzy at the top of the steps. "You look down there! We're moving all the furniture up here to check the floors again. Check the walls and woodwork too. Look for any hidden nooks. Maybe this house has nooks like mine does." She left the top of the steps to go back to the bedroom.

Jezabelle could hear furniture moving. She turned to Warbler. "You take the dining room." Turning to Phoebe, Jezabelle pointed to the kitchen. "Kitchen's yours, Phoebe; I'll take the living room and the bathroom."

"I'll take the sun porch and laundry room too," Phoebe volunteered.

"Pound on the walls and see if they sound hollow," "Warbler advised.

"Warbler, you read too many detective novels," Jezabelle scoffed.

"Pound on the walls and see if they sound hollow!" Miranda yelled from upstairs.

Warbler turned to Jezabelle. "And she writes them so she should know." He began to tap on the walls.

A loud crash came from the kitchen. "Ah, sorry! I'm fine; I just dropped a bottle of wrinkle cream that was in the cabinet. Rock uses wrinkle cream?" Phoebe's laughter echoed throughout the house.

Jezabelle pushed and shoved the furniture around the living room so she could see the floor. "Nothing here!" Jezabelle announced.

"Nothing upstairs either!" Lizzy added as she and Miranda came downstairs to join the others.

"Maybe the Brilliant brothers just decided to build a plain old house with this one," Phoebe suggested coming in from the kitchen, still holding the broken bottle of wrinkle cream.

"Rock has a basement. Maybe the clue's in the basement," Lizzy suggested.

"Or maybe in the attic. We never have investigated the attics since we found the clues on the first or second floor." Miranda moved to the steps.

"We know what's in our attics, but we don't know what's in Rock's or Annabelle's," Warbler concluded.

"Let's start with the basement. The outside basement entrance was taken out and sealed up a long time ago when the former owner lived here," Jezabelle told the group.

"Where's the basement door then?" Lizzy asked opening all the doors one by one. "These are all closets."

Jezabelle picked up her cell phone and shouted into it, "Rock!" She waited for him to answer. "I suppose just when we need him, he'll be busy at whatever work he does and not answer." She put the phone on speaker and waited.

"Hello."

"Rock, we're at your house. How do we get into your basement?" Lizzy yelled into the speaker of the phone.

"You... didn't... find... anything?"

"No, where's your basement door?" Warbler yelled from across the room so Rock could hear.

"Behind... the... coats."

Jezabelle wrinkled her nose. "Behind the coats?"

"The... closet... in the... living... room... with the... coats... in."

Lizzy looked in the closet. "All I see are coats, Rock."

"Move... the... coats and... slide... the wall... at the... back."

"You have a hidden door?" Phoebe threaded through the coats and peered into the back of the closet.

"Yup... former... owners... didn't... see any... need... to go... down... to the... basement... so... they built a... closet... in... front... of the... door. I... only use it... when... there's a... tornado warning."

Jezabelle began to take the coats out of the closet and hand them to Warbler.

"Rock, I ah... am sorry but we broke your bottle of wrinkle cream? Why do you use wrinkle cream? You're a guy." Jezabelle couldn't resist the little dig.

"Ah... I... ah... don't use... wrinkle... cream. It's... ah... ah... for... my snake. I... ah... ah... use... it... so... he doesn't... shed... his... skin."

"Wrinkle cream will keep a snake from shedding his skin?" Phoebe shook her head. "Makes sense. You learn something new every day."

"Rock, if we find something we'll let you know. Will you be home about ten?" Jezabelle's voice was muffled as one of the coats had stuck itself to her head and she was trying to get it untangled.

"I... will be... off... my... shift and... home... by ten. By... the... way don't... open... the... snake's... home... out in the... sunroom. He... can... be... cantankerous... at... times... if I... am... not there."

"I already saw him, Rock. He hissed. I made a face at him and left him alone. I've known some snakes in my time and I know enough to stay away from them." Phoebe moved to the phone Jezabelle had laid down in the living room so she could purge jackets. She popped the disconnect and turned to the group. "Jezabelle, you lead the way."

Jezabelle had just moved the pocket door to the side. "There are no lights. Phoebe, hand me my cell phone. You all might want to get yours out too to use your flashlight." Once she had her cell phone in her hand and turned on the flashlight feature, she aimed the light at the steps. "Careful, they are very rustic but I see a light pull cord at the bottom of the steps. I'll go first and turn it on." Carefully she moved down the stairs.

Once the light was on, the rest traversed the steps. "Just an old stone basement like the rest of ours," Warbler surmised.

"Mine's actually finished," Miranda informed the group.

"Really, did you do that?" Lizzy asked.

"No, it looks like it was done a long time ago when the house was built. Has excellent woodwork and walls."

Jezabelle touched the stone walls. "There's nothing down here. Doesn't everyone have stuff? Wouldn't the old owners leave something here? All that's here is the hot water heat furnace, though it's not the original boiler.

"And it's clean. Rock must keep it clean for whatever reason." Jezabelle moved to examine the walls. "Original stone walls."

"Well, if I had to go down to my basement during a tornado I'd keep it clean too," Phoebe interjected. "In fact, I dust mine to keep out the spiders but I keep some odds and ends down there, easier to go down one floor than to go up three to get to the attic."

Miranda moved to join Jezabelle. "I wonder." She moved her hands over the stone foundation. "I wonder if this house and maybe yours has some hidden nooks and crannies we haven't found. For instance, I had one stone brick in my fireplace that was a little loose. I pulled it out and there was a cubby behind it and in that cubby was a child's silver bracelet. I haven't figured out if there are more things hidden. It's another puzzle, I guess."

Jezabelle looked at Miranda. "So we could possibly be missing many things because we don't know what we're looking for, and they could be connected to this puzzle or another one."

"I'm beginning to think so." Miranda moved along the wall, peering closely.

"Everything's so gray," Mr. Warbler pointed out. "Almost silver, they didn't have silver rocks but it looks like the rocks in this basement have a shimmer."

"This house has to have a missing piece to our puzzle to find the treasure. I can't imagine they left one house out of the equation." Miranda tapped on a wall.

"Do you notice that these stones are all different sizes and shapes?" Mr. Warbler pointed to a row of small rocks and then large oblong-shaped rocks. He peered closely at the wall. "In fact, it looks like it's possible that there are two layers of stone here. I'm going to check something outside." He climbed the steps to the first floor.

"It's a big basement." Jezabelle stepped around the room.

"And it's all one room, which is unusual for these old houses," Mr. Warbler pointed out and then disappeared from view.

"We're wasting our time. I'm going to find Warbler." Phoebe put her foot on the steps just as Warbler reappeared, putting his foot on the top step.

"The outside is all large stone. So there are two layers in this basement," Warbler announced.

"And that helps us how?" Lizzy asked.

"It means that these stones could be covering something up." Miranda was already picking at a stone in the wall.

"Miranda, you can't take the basement apart." Phoebe grabbed her hand before Miranda pulled on a stone.

"But I can; look here!" Jezabelle pointed to a round stone she'd found in the corner up near the ceiling of the basement. "I can't reach it."

Miranda moved to help Jezabelle. She reached up but the stone wouldn't budge. Jezabelle was shining her light at the round object. "There's something etched in the stone. Can you read it, Miranda?"

Miranda stood on tiptoes and squinted at the stone as Jezabelle held her cell phone flashlight on the rock. "It says *Charity*."

"That's it! That's it! That's our ticket to the gold!" Phoebe was talking so fast the others had a hard time making out her words.

"Calm down, Phoebe." Lizzy grabbed her arm to keep her from jumping. "We don't know that."

Miranda reached into her pocket and took out a pocketknife.

"You have a knife?" Lizzy backed away.

"You didn't think we were going to come here unarmed after we've had all these floornappers, did you?" Miranda reached up with the knife and picked at the stone in the wall. When her soft picking didn't work, she stabbed the knife into the stone around the rock and the rock let loose and fell to the floor.

Jezabelle reached down and picked it up to examine it. "It's not a rock; it's a metal ball. We have a metal ball with the word *Charity* on it."

"Well, that gives a whole to meaning to our investigation. We don't have a ball and chain; we have a ball and key," Warbler joked.

"A key?" Lizzy was standing on her tiptoes squinting to see something in the hole left by the ball. "There's something still here." She reached up and took out an old piece of paper.

"What's it say? What's it say?" Phoebe moved to Lizzy and grabbed the note out of her hand.

"Yes, Phoebe, what does it say?" Jezabelle grabbed the note from Phoebe.

"*The key to understanding lies in the dropped ball.*"

"So do we drop the ball on the key?" Phoebe wondered.

"What key? You said you had a key?" Miranda was staring at the paper still held in Jezabelle's hands.

"Mr. Shifty brought us a key from the basement library. It, too, says *Charity*." Jezabelle dug in her pocket and showed the key to Miranda.

Mr. Warbler looked at his watch. "It's dinnertime. Let's go down and see what Jiffy has to eat. I might even imbibe a little after the morning we've had. This basement is giving me the heebie-jeebies."

"The what? Now he's making words up; we need to get him some food." Phoebe began to take Warbler's arm to lead him up the steps but before she could get to him, Lizzy had already scooped up his arm and was leading him upstairs.

"Warby you need to make sure you eat. Come with me. We can ride with Miranda."

Jezabelle twitched an eyebrow. She was going to have to ask her friend about this Warby business.

CHAPTER FORTY-NINE

"There's a table for all of us over there." Mr. Warbler pointed to a table by the window, hurried over, and sat down.

"I guess we're sitting there," Jezabelle announced.

Lizzy giggled. "I think Warby is hungry. This was a lot of exercise for him this morning." She took Jezabelle's arm and led her through the crowd. Miranda and Phoebe followed.

"Hey, there! Good to see we have the Penderghast Puzzle Protectors here with us today." Maddie, Jiffy's waitress, set water and menus down in front of the group. "Where's that cute Rock Stone? Isn't he a part of your group?"

Jezabelle frowned. "How do you know about us?"

"Well, you're famous and your pictures were in the paper. You're accused of being floornappers but then we see by the other article that that librarian, Marion, put in the paper that you started a puzzle group. Everyone wants to join!"

Jezabelle exchanged glances with the others in the group. Miranda said, "Yes, well we're not quite organized yet. We'll make sure you know when we're ready to accept applications to our group. I think I'll have the Jiffy Burger with fries and a piece of caramel apple pie."

"Me too!" Miranda set down her menu.

"I'll have the Jiffy Burger and fries, onion rings, and two pieces of pie. And Lizzy here will have the Jiffy Club Sandwich, a salad, and one of those pieces of pie is for her." Mr. Warbler turned and beamed at Lizzy who promptly blushed.

"I'll just have a glass of wine." Phoebe set her menu down. "And then you can add a chocolate tart to go with it."

"Where's Jiffy anyway?" Jezabelle asked. "He's usually putting out a fire in the oven."

"Oh," Maddie answered, "he's downstairs in his private rooms. We're not allowed down there. In fact, he locks himself in. I think he needs time away from the stress. And he seems to have this baking thing down pat. When we get here in the morning, all the delectable goodies are done." She took the menus and walked away.

"Where do we go from here?" Lizzy asked.

"We have a ball and a key and we have no idea if it fits anything. Honestly, my house has so many hidden tidbits that Braxton Brilliant hid for his kids it's hard to determine what fits our treasure hunt and what doesn't."

Jezabelle shook her head. "And who would know about what is possibly a treasure? The book in the library that Marion gave us would explain how anyone knew about our floors, but what led them to believe there might be a treasure?"

"Well, well, Jezzy, I see you and your friends are having a day out." Hank, Hanna, and Jeb stopped at their table. "What are you up to now?"

"Can't we have a lunch out?" Jezabelle sniffed, and feigned a hurt look.

"Miranda, I haven't seen you out this much since you moved here. Can't be getting too much work done on your book," Jeb addressed the author.

"The Penderghast neighborhood seems to be well represented. Where's Rock?" Hanna asked.

"We haven't seen him for a while. He's always working. Nice seeing you three, but we have the next puzzle to work on in the library. Have you heard our new name? The Lackadaisical Meandering."

"We have. Stay out of trouble!" Hank warned before the three proceeded to their table.

"Why would George Grifter have stolen the book out of the library and how would he know how to get into the safe? I always liked George," Jezabelle continued the conversation they had cut off when they were interrupted by the deputies.

"Here you go, folks!" Maddie arrived with the food, giving the right meal to the right person.

"You're good, Maddie. Jiffy got an ace waitress when he hired you," Warbler complimented the waitress.

"Tip of the day, Warbler, there's another piece of pie with your name on it to take home." She winked at the large man.

"Well, if it isn't my favorite Puzzle Protectors!" Marion Murkowsky gushed as she interrupted. I thought I might find you here when I couldn't get an answer at your home, Jezabelle."

"Let me know if you need anything else." Maddie moved away letting Marion continue.

Jezabelle addressed Marion's question. "Why were you calling? To tell me my cat was in your bushes again?"

"I'm so sorry if I was brusque this morning," Marion apologized. "I was befuddled. There was a key missing from the display case in the Brilliant Brothers' Room. I was dusting and had it in my hand when I went down to the basement and, when your cats surprised me, I must have dropped it. I went back after I called you and I couldn't find it anywhere. You didn't happen to see it? Maybe the cat got it and dragged it into the bushes. I looked there too after you left."

Jezabelle and the others put their heads down and concentrated on their food. In between bites, Jezabelle answered, "I–didn't-see-any-key-while-I-was-in-the-bushes."

"Well, if you hear of anyone finding it let me know." Marion gave a wave before going to the counter, picking up her coffee, then leaving the Bistro.

"You lied," Phoebe whispered to Jezabelle.

"I didn't. I didn't see the key while I was in the bushes. I didn't see the key until I got out from under the bushes and saw you," Jezabelle whispered back.

"Look! There's Junior coming out of the back room! Why would he be in Jiffy's back room?" Lizzy questioned.

"He has a package. Looks like it could be a pie. He's probably getting a pie to share for coffee break at the Intelligent Icicle Factory."

"I have news!" Lizzie announced. "I bought Annabelle's house! I got it for a song because it was on the market for at least two years and apparently since it had been burglarized and someone had died there, no one wanted to risk buying it."

Beaming, Jezabelle turned to Lizzy. "We're going to be neighbors! We're going to have so much fun."

"So have you met your garage neighbor?" Phoebe asked.

"No, it's the strangest thing. Fleck says that he couldn't tell me who owned it. It's in the contract that it has to stay secret. Maybe I'll find out when I live there. I'll peer out of my tower window and spy on my neighbor."

A cough, then a choking sound, and Warbler pushed himself back from the table, interrupting the conversation. "Ah, excuse me, I swallowed wrong. I have to go."

Concerned, Lizzy stood up to go after him. "Warby, are you okay? Can we drive you?"

He waved her away as he rushed for the door. "No, I'll find my own way! I'll see you all later." He coughed, sputtered, and left.

"Now that was strange," Lizzy said as she sat back down.

Miranda rolled her eyes. "Well, Lizzy, you'll find the Penderghast neighborhood is a strange neighborhood and all is not as it seems."

Phoebe frowned at Miranda. "That sounds *puzzling*."

"Well, *that's* what we're here for," Miranda answered. "The pieces will come together," she said knowingly, a glint of mischief showing in her eyes.

CHAPTER FIFTY

The stars were shining and the moon was bright as Jezabelle and Lizzy had a late-night glass of wine on her upstairs porch.

"I love this porch and this neighborhood," Lizzie sighed. "And to think we can do this more often now that I'll live here soon."

"I'm glad you decided to spend the night. You never did tell us why Miranda had to pick you up."

"Someone slashed my tires," Lizzy answered nonchalantly.

"No one slashes tires in Brilliant. Are you sure you just didn't run over something?" Jezabelle remembered an earlier escapade when Lizzy thought someone had stolen her car. She'd called the police only to find that she'd forgotten that the garage was going to come and get her car for maintenance and it was at the shop getting fixed.

"No, HH said someone slashed my tires. Actually, he said I'd been hanging around with you too long and that was starting to appear to be dangerous. But he was teasing. He thought it was some kids out for a prank."

Jezabelle took another sip of wine. "Isn't the big dipper beautiful tonight? I love summer."

Lizzy agreed before changing the subject. "Rock didn't seem too surprised that we found something in his house. Didn't you think that was strange?"

Jezabelle shook her head. "No, he was after cheesecake and Rock never seems to get excited about anything. At least he didn't mind us snooping at his house."

"A lot of good it did us. There are just too many clues and too many loose ends. We aren't any closer to solving this puzzle, but at least no one else has been killed, except for Fred Rally."

"And he was killed in your newly bought house," Jezabelle reminded her. "Doesn't that bother you? Lizzy you can't move in until the crime is solved. It wouldn't be safe."

"I sold my house and I have to move next week," Lizzy informed her.

"You can stay here until it's solved."

"It might never be solved, Jezabelle. I can't live here forever. I'll be fine, and, besides, I'll have my mysterious garage neighbor in my backyard. I went over and knocked on his door, but everything is locked up tight and there was no answer. Do you ever see anyone back there? You can see across all the yards from here."

The only person I've ever seen in your backyard is Warbler. And according to Phoebe who followed Miranda on her run one night, the other person was Miranda arguing with Warbler in the middle of the night."

A perplexed look spread across Lizzy's face. "Why would Warbler and Miranda be meeting in my backyard?"

"Good question to which I've tried to get an answer but we always get interrupted. Look!" Jezabelle pointed to Rock's driveway. "She's here again?"

"Who's she? It's two in the morning. Does she come every night at two?" Lizzy peered into the darkness.

"I snuck back and got a closer look. I think it looks like Hanna."

"What would Hanna be doing at Rock's at this hour? When does she leave?" Lizzy leaned over the railing to get a better look.

Jezabelle pulled her back. "You don't want her to see you."

"Why not?" Lizzy sat back in her chair.

"I don't know. Do you think I should tell HH?"

"Look!" Lizzy pointed to Annabelle's house. "See that! It looks like a soft light in Annabelle's basement."

"Your basement now." Jezabelle looked to where Lizzy was pointing.

"It does appear to be a soft light. Maybe it's shining off the windows and the light is really outside." Lizzy squinted her eyes to see if it would help her pinpoint what she was seeing.

"It's moving. How would they get in the basement without us seeing them? We would see the movement outside lifting the cellar door up. Wouldn't we?" Jezabelle stood up and leaned over the railing to get a better look.

"We were just in the basement a couple of days ago. It was well kept, but there was nothing there except for some empty shelves where Annabelle must have kept canning supplies. Remember her daughter said she was always trying to get into the basement to get some of her jars of canned goods? Let's go!" Lizzy grabbed Jezabelle's arm.

"You want to go over there?"

"It's my house now and I have the key. I got it early since no one lives there. I have permission to move things into the house. Annabelle's family lives out east and they aren't coming back. They cleared it out years ago."

"Lizzy, welcome to the Penderghast neighborhood and its ghosts."

"Look!" Lizzy pointed. "The light went away."

"Do you want to wait until morning to investigate?"

Lizzy giggled. "Do you remember zombie hunting in the woods when we were young? It's been a long time since we pretended there were zombies. Let's go find zombies in our old age." Lizzy was down the steps before Jezabelle could answer.

Leaving Jezabelle's back door unlocked, the two women stepped out onto her back porch. "Do you think we can make it without turning on our cell flashlights?" Jezabelle gripped her phone tightly.

"The moon lights the backyard. We don't want anyone to see us. Wouldn't it be funny if we ran into Warbler since you said you've seen him in Annabelle's backyard." Lizzy's giggle tickled Jezabelle's funny bone and she too giggled.

"Maybe it's him. Maybe we don't know him as well as we thought we did. Maybe he killed Fred. He *was* in the backyard that night," Jezabelle informed Lizzy.

"Not Warby. He wouldn't hurt a flea. I'm sure he has a good explanation." Linking arms, Jezabelle and Lizzy moved slowly across Rock's backyard, keeping an eye on Rock's house to make sure Rock and the mysterious woman weren't watching. Reaching Annabelle's yard, they stopped behind a bush.

"Don't see any light through the windows now. Maybe we imagined it," Lizzy whispered.

"I guess the coast is clear. Miranda's lights are off in her house and in all the rest of the houses too. Are you sure we want to look at this now?"

"We saw lights, Jezabelle, in Annabelle's, or I mean, my basement. If someone was in my basement in the middle of the night I want to know about it." Lizzy moved forward toward the outside cellar door.

Jezabelle followed Lizzy. She turned and whispered, "The padlock's still in place. Hand me the key."

Lizzy handed Jezabelle the key and then dug in her pocket and pulled out a steak knife.

"You stole a steak knife from my house? Why?" Jezabelle asked as she lifted the cellar door.

"To protect us. We used to use sticks when we were pretending to zombie hunt when we were kids but this might be a real zombie so I brought a knife. If Miranda can carry a knife, so can I."

Jezabelle turned on her flashlight and shone it down to the bottom of the steps. "She uses her knife for research. You use that knife to carve a steak. Put it down—it's all dark down there." She carefully took one step at a time down the rustic steps. Lizzy held on to Jezabelle's shirt to follow her.

At the bottom of the steps, Lizzy turned on her light. "There's no one here," she whispered holding on to Jezabelle for courage.

They shuffled across the floor moving slowly and together. Jezabelle shone the light into the corner where they had found the window open when they'd examined the basement on Lizzy's house tour with Fleck. "Window's shut."

Lizzy was shining her light around the rest of the basement. "Something isn't right but I can't quite put my finger on it."

Jezabelle moved to the shelf in the middle of the floor. "Weren't these shelves empty when we were here before?" Jezabelle picked up a jar of canned pickles.

Lizzy moved to Jezabelle's side. "These are green beans." She lifted up a second jar.

"Whoever canned these really packed 'em in tight." Jezabelle shook the jar and nothing inside moved.

"Someone did a lot of canning in a short time," Lizzy surmised. "Maybe Annabelle didn't imagine the jars she was always trying to get down in the basement to use."

"But who did this and how? Feel—these jars of pickles are still warm as if they just came out of a water bath." Jezabelle handed the jar to Lizzy. "We did see light down here but how did they get in?"

Lizzy shone her flashlight around the walls. "Nothing except for those empty shelves over there in the corner where we found that old note stuck under it." She moved closer to the shelf.

Jezabelle followed, stopping first to pull the chain on the basement light. "Wiggle the shelf, Lizzy."

Lizzy touched the side of the shelf and gave it a push. "It's solid. Really solid."

"Here. I'll stand on this side and pull and you stand on the other side and see if we can lift it out from the wall." The shelf held tight and wouldn't move.

"So much for that theory. It's kind of silly thinking there was a secret door." Lizzy, tired from pushing, sat down on the cement floor. "I'm too old for this."

"This is Brilliant and the Brilliant brothers loved puzzles. It would be just like them from what we know. Not silly at all."

"The police must have checked this basement out with a fine-toothed comb when Fred died," Lizzy pointed out.

"But they didn't know at that time what we know now." Jezabelle was still examining the shelf. "It's like the back is stuck to the wall."

Lizzy stood back up and used her light to examine the inside of the shelves. Giving up, she turned to speak to Jezabelle using the shelves as a backrest to lean on. The shelves moved and she fell backward into the frame of the shelf.

"The shelves move. That's it!" Jezabelle pulled Lizzy out of the casing and began pushing all the shelves in. They fell through slits in the wall making a large racket.

Lizzy's wide eyes gazed at the back of the shelf. "I hope no one heard that." She pulled out her knife from her pocket.

"Put the knife away, Lizzy! That's a hidden door. The shelves are double-sized so they stuck out the same length on the other side so someone could take them out and then open the frame of the bookshelf and open the door. See the hinges behind the shelves?"

Jezabelle pulled the frame out swinging it into the room opening the cabinet door, revealing a small dark tunnel.

"Don't you think we should call someone? Like HH? Or Warby?" Lizzy suggested.

"And tell them what? We found another hidden door and a few jars of pickles. We have our phones and we can call someone if we need to. Let's go zombie-hunting and see where this leads." Jezabelle's excited voice made Lizzy feel better.

Jezabelle took the lead, shining her cell phone light ahead of them. Lizzy held onto Jezabelle as she too joined her light with Lizzy's.

"Can you see anything? It's just a tunnel. Where do you think we're going? It's really an old tunnel. There don't seem to be any spiders. All stone, like our basements. Kind of rough. Do you see anything up ahead?" Lizzy's nervous mutterings continued. "Do you suppose this was part of the underground network for hiding slaves?"

"No. Brilliant was founded after that. I think this is one of the Brilliant brothers' fun puzzles. Quit yammering; we don't know where this is leading or who's on the other side," Jezabelle instructed.

"Jezabelle, I think we need to call Hank and I'm going to do it right now." She looked at her phone. "Or maybe when we get out of here since I don't have any signal. How far have we gone?"

Instead of answering, Jezabelle tripped and with a thump landed on the dirt floor. Lizzy went down with her since she'd been holding on tightly to Jezabelle's arm.

Lizzy lifted herself off Jezabelle and reached down to help Jezabelle up. "Are you hurt? What happened?"

"I caught the edge of something along the side of the wall that I must have missed with my flashlight." She swung the flashlight to her side.

Lizzy gasped. "It's the piece from your floor. See! Here are the squares and here is the x!"

Jezabelle put the light on the piece of hardwood and then swung the light down the side of the tunnel ahead of them. "And there are the rest of the pieces."

Walking slowly, they examined each piece.

Lizzy pointed to the last larger piece that reached to the top of the side of the tunnel. "It's the map from the library wall. Jezabelle, where does this lead, and who did this? Maybe we should go back and call Hank or the others."

"Shh, let's keep going and see where this leads. But we need to be quiet in case whoever this is, is waiting at the end. It hasn't been long since we saw that light. When we find out where this leads, we'll go back and call Hank and the police. And Lizzy— now might be a good time to get your knife out."

CHAPTER FIFTY-ONE

Jezabelle and Lizzy moved slowly through the old tunnel making sure not to trip on any more surprises they might find along the way.

"This is a long tunnel, don't you think?" Lizzy peered into the darkness ahead.

"It might seem like that. I think we've only gone a few blocks, maybe a mile," Jezabelle concluded.

Lizzy pulled Jezabelle to a stop. "Look! There's a light up ahead. Turn off our lights; we can find our way to the light." Lizzy giggled at her words. "Well let's hope it's not the big light in the sky if we encounter any zombies."

Carefully, they moved forward. "It's a door that's been left open," Jezabelle whispered.

They quietly proceeded to the open door, but held back so they couldn't be seen. "I don't see anyone," Lizzy said.

"Me either, but they might come back. Let's take a quick peek, get out of here, and call HH." Jezabelle slowly moved forward, sticking her head around the corner of the door. "It's one large room but no one's there."

Lizzy moved through the doorway. "It's a kitchen and a storage room for flour," she said, noticing all the bags of flour on the shelves.

"Look! There's more canning jars. It looks like they ran out of room for storage." Jezabelle eyed the jars on the shelf.

"Where are we?" Lizzy moved to the basement window that was covered with a blackout curtain. She lifted the curtain. "It's still dark out. I can see some lights."

Jezabelle moved to her side and stepped on a chair that was under the window. "We're in Jiffy's basement—the basement of the Brilliant Bistro."

Lizzy gasped and dropped the curtain. "Jiffy's behind all this?"

Jezabelle looked around the room. "Why does he have a kitchen downstairs when he has one upstairs? Do you suppose this is the room no one's allowed in?" She moved to the inside door to open it. It wouldn't budge. "It's locked so I guess this is the room."

"We need to go and call Hank and Hanna." Lizzy moved toward the tunnel but Jezabelle stuck out a hand to stop her.

"And tell them what? That we decided to investigate a tunnel in the middle of the night because we found jars of pickles in your basement and now we found more pickles and flour?"

"What about your floor pieces? We need to go. Jiffy might be back soon. Listen, I hear voices upstairs."

Jezabelle put her ear to the door. "Jiffy is talking to a woman. They're at the top of the stairs. It sounds like Miranda."

"It's four-thirty. What is Miranda doing here at this time of morning? Oh, wait! Remember she said she used to come in and help with the baking when Fred was here. Maybe she's doing that now."

"Lizzy, I can guarantee you Miranda isn't doing any baking for Jiffy." Jezabelle turned and eyed the kitchen. "He's busy right now so let's do a little snooping and get out of here. You listen at the door in case you hear him coming."

Lizzy moved toward the door and put her ear to the metal. "It's kind of interesting that this old building has a metal door."

Jezabelle was moving around the room looking in drawers and cupboards. "All canning and baking supplies here." She moved over to an old desk in the corner of the room and began to rummage in the drawers. "Nothing here either."

"Sometimes those old desks had false bottoms. If there is one, there would be a latch in the drawer right under the desktop," Lizzy advised. "I used to have a desk similar to that. It was my ex-husband's father's wife's mother's grandmother's."

"What?"

"Never mind; check it out to see if there's a false bottom."

Jezabelle rummaged around in the drawer right under the middle of the desk. "Got it." The latch moved and the bottom of the drawer popped up. "It's a book!" She lifted it out of the drawer.

Lizzy, forgetting her post by the door, moved to look over Jezabelle's shoulder. "It looks similar to the book Marion gave us."

"This is the book that will solve our puzzle. Look! It has diagrams and on the first page it says, *The treasure is yours for those who are willing to look for the rainbow*," Jezabelle read.

Lizzy reached over and turned the next page. "It lists the Brilliant brothers' names and the three wives' names and the clues to solve the puzzle. Jiffy had this book all along. This is the book we need to solve the puzzle."

Jezabelle grabbed the book and said, "We need to get out of here and take this to Hank. This is the

proof we need. I can't believe Jiffy would do this."
Jezabelle turned to leave but stumbled on the corner
of a shelf knocking a bag of flour to the floor,
tearing it and spilling its contents. She heard Lizzy
gasp.

"I don't suppose those are rhinestones." Lizzy
was looking at a pile of sparkling gems that had
spilled out with the flour.

"No, Lizzy, they are *not* rhinestones. How nice
of you to visit me. Were you bringing me more
baked goods, sweetie Jezabelle?"

The women turned to see Jiffy Jacks in the
doorway with a gun pointed straight at them.
Behind him was Rock Stone.

"Jiffy, you need them. They have the key and the
ball they found in my basement and the last clue.
We need to take them out to the cemetery and find
the gold. Oh, and take that steak knife sticking out
of Lizzy's pocket." Rock moved further into the
room.

Lizzy's mouth was hanging wide open in
astonishment at seeing Rock Stone with Jiffy Jacks,
while Jezabelle was sputtering with anger. "Rock
Stone, what happened to the "I... work... late...
but... and we have to wait for ever to listen to you
speak and you're in on this? You pretended to be
working with us?"

Rock laughed. "I did. We were having trouble
putting the pieces together but when you got
involved, you seemed to come up with more clues
than we could find. And, of course, our dolt of a
police chief and his crew couldn't find the broad
side of a barn."

Lizzy looked down at the floor. "And the
diamonds; you're smuggling diamonds?"

Rock moved Lizzy away from the spilled flour and diamonds. He picked up a few of the spilled diamonds and held them out for Lizzy to see. "Beautiful aren't they? That's why I came to town––to help Jiffy, but when Jiffy here found this old book in a secret drawer in the old bar, we decided to expand our operations. Unfortunately, old Fred decided to take up residence in Annabelle's house while he was baking for Jiffy and caught us hiding the diamonds in the basement. It just so happened it was around the time that we were trying to put the floor pieces together and well… you know the rest."

Jiffy shook his head while keeping the gun trained on the women. "Yup, Karma. It was a shame; he was a great baker." Jiffy smiled. "And he didn't know that we took some of the baking supplies down here. We baked up some goodies, stuck some diamonds in them to hide them and kept them here in the basement. Fred always thought the help was stealing the baked goods. Poor Fred, he's dead, and, by the way, did you know I'm wed?"

Footsteps could be heard coming down the steps. "Jiffy, dear, it's not like you to be careless and leave this door open." Marion stopped when she saw Lizzy and Jezabelle. "Well, look what we have here—the Penderghast Puzzle Protectors, at least two of them. Junior, dear, help your father tie these two women up."

"Father?" Lizzy spouted.

"Jezabelle, Lizzy, meet my wife Marion and my son Junior." Jiffy, still holding the gun on the women, hugged his wife.

"Where's the key?" Marion asked Jezabelle.

"I don't have it with me," Jezabelle answered.

"No, she gave it to the police," Lizzy added.

Rock Stone looked Lizzy straight in the eye. "You're lying. Where are the key and the ball? We know you have them. We want them now."

"We don't have them," Jezabelle insisted.

Rock picked up his phone. "Miranda... I... know... it's... early... but I... just... got a... call... from... Jezabelle... and she... said... to... call... the others... and... bring the... key... and... the... ball... and meet us—"

Jezabelle began to speak but Junior put a hand over her mouth at the same time Marian did the same with Lizzy. Rock continued.

"at the... the old... Mudd... farm. We... think... we know... where... the... treasure... is." Rock listened for a minute as Miranda spoke.

"No... don't... call... Hank... until we... have... it... solved. It's... almost... light... you... should... be... able to... make... your way... on... the... path... without any... flashlight. And... Lizzy... is... with Jezabelle." He hung up his phone. "Time to go." He pulled out his gun and trained it on Lizzy. No funny business you two or you'll never know the answer to the mystery. And I know you couldn't die before knowing the answer to the puzzle."

"The outside basement door opens to the alley; no one's ever back there," Jiffy advised, pushing Jezabelle toward the door.

"Jezabelle, don't forget that there's truth in the unseen." Rock finished the statement with a wink.

CHAPTER FIFTY-TWO

Lizzy whispered to Jezabelle from the backseat of the van, "What did Rock mean when he said there's truth in the unseen?"

"I think it was his way of telling us he wasn't going to kill us," Jezabelle answered.

"You think so?"

"No... I have no idea. I think we'll have lots of time to ponder that statement." Jezabelle hollered up to the front of the van, "If we're going to help you solve this puzzle, tell us how you found out. After all, if you do what you're planning to do, we'll take the secret with us just like the Brilliant brothers."

Lizzy nudged Jezabelle with her elbow. "Don't give them any ideas."

Jiffy laughed. "Aw, Jezabelle sweetie, I loved visiting you every night. But all good things must come to an end. I guess we can let you in on our secrets."

"Honey, tell her why we came to Brilliant in the first place," Marion urged. "It's such a sweet story."

Jiffy reached across to the passenger seat and patted Marion's cheek. "Well, my Marion, my little librarian, got the job at the library at the same time I bought the Brilliant Bistro and remodeled it. You see, we needed someplace to hide our real business. Have you ever heard of blood diamonds? We— should I say I?—deal in blood diamonds."

"Yes, it was the perfect business for us. We would smuggle the diamonds in with the flour and then we'd hide them in the baked goods in our downstairs' freezer or in the pickles we canned. The goods were hid in the middle of the goods, so to speak," Marion continued.

"I found the tunnel when I was remodeling the Bistro. Apparently, Barton Brilliant owned the Bistro and lived in Annabelle's house. He built the tunnel so he could get back and forth between his business in the winter and during the night when he did his baking. It was all documented in the book you found. I followed the tunnel to Annabelle's house. She never used the basement, so it was the perfect place for me to store the canned goods with the diamonds in them. At one time, there was an old freezer down there, but when Annabelle's family put the house up for sale they got rid of the old freezer so my pies had to be stashed down in my basement. I had to move fast when I heard it had been sold and get all my goods out of there."

"That explains the diamonds but what about our floors you stole," Jezabelle asked. "We found them in the tunnel."

"We decided to do that when we found the book," Junior's excited voice added to the discussion. He now held his father's gun and still had it trained on the women from his middle seat in the van.

"We decided to collect all the pieces from the floors and put them together side by side in the tunnel and along with the map it led us to the Mudd farm. Braxton's, Barton's and Bennet's wives were sisters and their maiden name was Mudd. The three Brilliant brothers married the Mudd sisters. And the clues on the papers we found were enough to lead us to the cemetery." Jiffy became lost in his story. "We planted Junior out on the farm in the house to see what he could find. If he was living there, he had access to the entire farm. We actually planned on buying the farm."

"So how did the house burn down?" Lizzy asked.

Junior squirmed in his seat. "I ah, burned it down."

Marion swatted Junior on the arm, almost making him drop his gun. Rock Stone, seeing Junior's hand jump, tightened his grip on the gun he too held on the women.

"My Junior boy has a bad temper and he got mad because he wasn't finding anything. He picked up an oil lamp he was using and smashed it on the ground and then took a stick and took the flames and lit the curtains on fire. He didn't get his brains from me," Marion admonished.

"Yah, well I forgot the book. Thought it had burned up and then we saw George Grifter sitting at the counter of the Brilliant Bistro paging through the book. Said he found it in the fire and was going to turn it over to the police." Junior laughed.

Jiffy pulled into the driveway of the Mudd farm and cut the engine. "The others aren't here yet so I guess we have time to finish the story. After all, soon you won't be able to tell anyone and we'll have moved on to greener pastures."

Marion rubbed her hands together in anticipation of telling the rest of the story. "Well, my lovely hubby Jiffy took George Grifter some soup that day when he was on duty, only it was laced with peanut dust. He knew George was very allergic to peanut dust. He removed the evidence of the soup and then took the book we needed and planted the book we actually found in the safe in the library to make it look like George was the perpetrator."

"Hank said George died of a heart attack." Jezabelle popped the fact into the conversation. "He knew he didn't die of a heart attack, but the police are keeping it quiet.

"They questioned me and I told them about the soup but I told them it must have come in contact with the peanut dust without me knowing it." Jiffy's tone held pride at the subterfuge.

"It's time you two were quiet," Rock Stone ordered.

"You can't kill us all. The rest of the neighborhood is coming. You can't kill us all," Lizzy blustered.

"You and Jezabelle will be in the empty graves. They've already been dug up so no one will suspect bodies were put back in the grave and as for the others—tell them Marion," Jiffy instructed.

"Your friends came looking for you two but poor Mr. Warbler fell in the pond and the others died saving him. Don't worry, we'll make it painless," Marion assured them.

"The others are here!" Jiffy got out of the truck and indicated to Rock and Junior that they should bring the women.

"Jiffy, what are you doing here? Rock, are we close to finding the treasure?" Phoebe's excited voice droned on until she saw the guns in their hands.

Miranda skewered Rock with her eyes. "I knew you weren't what you said you were."

Seeing Jezabelle and Lizzy being led out of the truck, she immediately went to their side.

"You two," Rock said, shaking the gun at Mr. Warbler and Phoebe, "get over by them."

"Did you bring the key and the ball?" Rock asked Miranda.

"You can talk like the rest of us! That was fake too!" She reached up her hand to punch him, remembered the gun, and backed down. Taking the ball and key out of her heavy tote, she gave it to him.

"Let's go, folks. We need to find the rainbow." Jiffy indicated they should start walking down the path. "Junior, lead the way."

The group moved down the path with Junior leading and Jiffy Jacks bringing up the rear. When they reached the clearing by the cemetery, they moved the group close to the lake and around the hedge.

Junior was the first around the hedge, wading a little into the water. He disappeared from view. Mr. Warbler and then Marion were next around.

Jezabelle heard a grunt from Warbler. She thought it sounded like he'd fallen. Miranda, Lizzy, and Phoebe were huddled together as they went around the hedge.

Rock Stone hung back and said to Jiffy, "I'll keep an eye. You go first."

Jiffy moved past Rock. Quickly, Rock followed, holding his gun as he slipped around the corner of the hedge to the cemetery. Laughter bubbled in his throat.

Hanna and Hank Hardy had Jiffy Jacks handcuffed on the ground. Jeb Jardene had Junior's gun in his hands, while Stick Straight was handcuffing a protesting Marion.

"I see you don't need me, Hank—you've got it under control. Jezabelle, these four members of your honorable police department are the unseen. They were watching all along." Rock walked over and looked Jiffy straight in the face. "What a shame, Jiff! Maybe we should start calling you Jailbird Jacks because that's what you're going to be."

Jezabelle and the Penderghast Puzzle Protectors watched as the Brilliant Police Department led Jiffy, Marion, and Junior away. Rock Stone stayed behind with the Puzzle Protectors.

"Can I still be in your group?" he asked with a twinkle in his eye.

"We still haven't solved the puzzle," Jezabelle pointed out. "I guess we need all the help we can get."

Miranda, instead of paying attention to the banter, was looking closely at the headstones. "These are pretty worn." She began to use her sleeve to brush off the tops of the stones. "Look! There are some grooves in the top of Charity's stone."

The others huddled around the stone and looked closely at the top of the stone.

Rock asked Miranda, "Do you have your pocket knife?"

She felt in her pocket. "Oh, my gosh, I forgot I had it. I could have used it!" She pulled it out of her pocket.

Rock held out his hand for the knife, opened it, and began scraping the years of crud off the top of the stone.

Lizzy peered closely at it. "It does look like a rainbow and it goes down the sides of the stone."

"Are the others like that?" Phoebe moved to Hope's stone. "Doesn't look like there's anything on that one."

"The only name we've ever seen on the clues with the rainbow is *Charity*." Jezabelle pointed out.

Rock kept scraping. "Yup. Looks like it could have been a rainbow at one time, colored and everything."

They all stared at the monument.

"Well where's the gold?" Phoebe started trying to jiggle the stone.

"What does the ball and key have to do with it? Think puzzle-like," Warbler told them. "Maybe they are pieces to a puzzle and the gravestone is the puzzle board."

"It's a good thing the sun's shining; we don't have to use flashlights anymore," Lizzy added.

"How did you two get into this mess?" Miranda asked.

"We'll explain later. Let's look for the gold at the end of the rainbow."

Mr. Warbler was closely examining the monument. He ran his hands over the sides. "Look, here it is on the side. It's an indentation. Where's the key?"

Miranda handed him the key as the others gathered around. He took the key and it hooked perfectly and tight in the indentation of the monument. They heard it click in place.

"Now what? Nothing happened?" An impatient Phoebe clapped her hands together.

"Give me that ball." Jezabelle held out her hand for Miranda to drop the steel ball into her hand. "Watch this." She reached down to the base of the monument and ran her hand over a round indentation in it. She lifted her hand high and dropped the steel ball. It hit its mark in the hold. They heard another click.

Rock tentatively put his hand on the monument. It was loose. He got down on his knees to where the top of the monument touched the base. Taking the pocketknife, he slid it between the top and bottom stone and felt a piece of metal. He gave it a push and the side of the monument came loose from the bottom stone. He did this on all four sides of the monument.

Jezabelle, Miranda, Lizzy, Phoebe, and Warbler each took hold of the bottom of the monument on all sides and lifted it up. They all gasped at one time, realizing the outside was a stone cover.

"It's gold! It really is gold!" Phoebe's eyes glazed over.

The others reached in to touch the gold that had been melted into the shape of the monument.

"Well, my friends, you've solved the puzzle and found the gold at the end of the rainbow. The Brilliant Brothers would be proud." Rock Stone bowed to his friends. Sure you don't want to join my agency?" he teased.

"And what agency might that be, Rock Stone?" Jezabelle ran her hands over the gold tombstone.

"The FBI."

CHAPTER FIFTY-THREE

"Say *gold*!" Snoop Steckle said to the Penderghast Puzzle Protectors before he snapped their picture.

"Gold!" they all shouted before they heard the click of his camera.

"Perfect picture for the front page of the *Brilliant Times Chronicle*. You'll be famous the world over. What's next for this group?" he continued his interview.

They all started talking at one time. "One at time. Jezabelle, you first."

"We've hardly had time to digest our little escapade yesterday so we choose not to comment."

Phoebe added, "We have many more puzzles in us."

"Does that mean you know of something else tawdry going on in Brilliant?" Snoop questioned.

Jezabelle answered for Phoebe, "No, it means we're going inside my house and have some coffee and baked goods. If you want to call my baked goods tawdry then go right ahead. Thanks for the interview, Snoop." She and Lizzy grabbed Phoebe and pushed her off the porch, through the door into Jezabelle's foyer.

"Kind of rude, wasn't it?" Mr. Warbler asked, following them in.

"He can have another scoop when my book is done," Miranda added.

"Make yourselves at home. I made a raspberry pear cheesecake for the occasion. I have an announcement to make!" Jezabelle went into her kitchen to get the cheesecake. Lizzy began to pour the coffee.

"Where's Rock? Is he no longer part of us?" Phoebe asked.

Jezabelle answered, coming into the room with the cheesecake. "He'll be here, along with Hank and Hanna. Hank said he'd fill us in on all the details, not that they have it all sorted out yet."

"What's your announcement, Jezabelle?" Miranda purred as she took her first bite of cheesecake.

Jezabelle stood up straight and Lizzy joined her. They hooked arms. "When everything is straightened out, Lizzy and I are going to buy and run the Brilliant Bistro!"

"I'm really going to gain weight; I can't resist your baking." Warbler ran his hands together in anticipation.

"Warby?" Lizzy sweetly addressed the overweight man. "I think you and I will have to work on some special low-calorie sweets for you." Lizzy left Jezabelle's side and sat down next to him giving him a hug.

"You know, Warbler, while we're waiting for Brilliant's finest to fill us in, it's time to tell us what you and Miranda were doing together in Annabelle's backyard the night Fred Rally was killed." Jezabelle sat down and nodded to Miranda.

"Yes, it's time you told them the truth," Miranda told Warbler. "Or I will."

"Well, ah… we… uh, were arguing."

"Arguing about what, Warby? It's okay; we know you didn't kill Fred." Lizzy patted his arm.

"Miranda found out my secret. She'd been out for a jog, came back through the trails, and saw us."

Warbler lowered his head and snuck a glance at Lizzy.

"Us? Who?" Lizzy's face puckered into a frown.

"Ah, ah, me and Phoebe's mother."

Phoebe jumped up, advancing on Warbler. "My mother? You and my mother are meeting in the middle of the night!"

Jezabelle jumped up and put herself in between Warbler and Phoebe. "Calm down, Phoebe, there must be a good explanation. Go on." She nodded to Warbler.

Warbler looked at Miranda. "Well, we couldn't meet at her house because of your sister and we didn't want you to know what we were doing yet." He turned his gaze to Phoebe.

"My mother!" Phoebe again shouted.

Miranda decided things were getting a little out of hand. "Relax, it's not what you think, although that is what I thought too."

"Well, what is it?" Phoebe, still agitated, moved back and sat down.

"Tell them who you really are, Warbler," Miranda coaxed.

"Who you really are? Warby, you are Warby?" Lizzy moved her hand off his shoulder.

"Well, no one seems to be who they are in this neighborhood, except me." Jezabelle's disgruntled tone wasn't lost on the others.

"I'll tell them. You have heard of Marcus Rinaldo, the famous portrait and landscape artist." Miranda got up and with a sweeping of her arm toward Warbler she said, "Meet Marcus Rinaldo, Portrait and Landscape Artist and your neighbor, Lizzie."

Lizzie stood up. "You're Marcus Rinaldo?"

Warbler hung his head, nodding at the same time.

"And you didn't tell us? Why?" Jezabelle asked.

"Well, I just wanted to be treated like everyone else when I moved here. My picture's not out there, and I've always tried to keep my identity secret. I send someone else to pretend to be me at my shows so no one knows what I look like. I paint better if I'm anonymous. I bought the garage cottage so I can paint and that's why I go back and forth in the middle of the night. Miranda just so happened to catch me when Phoebe's mother was leaving my studio one night. She's having a portrait painted for her children."

"She knows who you are?" Phoebe asked.

"No, she just thinks I'm someone who paints pictures." He smiled. "And none of you are going to tell anyone my secret. Right, Miranda?"

The Penderghast Puzzle Protectors glanced at each other and then Lizzy said, "We're the Penderghast Puzzle Protectors and we protect one another. Right, everyone?"

"Right!" they all shouted.

"I won't even tell my sister, that my mother's been sneaking out at night. She's not like me, she'd freak!"

"Shh, Hank and Hanna and Rock are here." Jezabelle warned, moving to the door to open it before they rang the doorbell.

"Good; you're all here," Hank said, handing a vase of roses to Jezabelle. "These were on your porch."

Hanna had a glint in her eye. "Maybe that's why you were always up when I'd visit Rock at two in the morning."

"Yes, Jezzy read the card. It seems I have another puzzle to solve. Who's your mystery admirer?" Hank peered over her shoulder to read the card.

Phoebe grabbed the card out of Jezabelle's hand. "Sweetie, Roses are Red, Violets are blue, solving the crime, I'm so proud of you."

Jezabelle blushed and grabbed the card back. "Hank, let's hear the scoop."

"Not so fast," Phoebe interrupted, grabbing the card back. "The only person I ever heard call you *sweetie* was Jiffy Jacks."

"Jezabelle grabbed the card back from Phoebe. "Jiffy wasn't sweet on me. When Fred died, I started doing some baking for him at the Brilliant Bistro. He'd come by and pick up what I'd baked and, occasionally, I'd meet him at the Mudd farm that I then didn't know was the Mudd farm, so no one would know I was his baker."

"And he's now in jail with no way to call in flowers," Hank added. "It appears the Puzzle Protectors have another puzzle to solve. Who's sweet on Jezabelle? Who is it, Jezzy? This old friend would like to know."

"Enough about my flowers. I want to know how Rock became involved in this and why you're sneaking into Rock's in the middle of the night, Hanna?" Jezabelle put the spotlight on her neighbor.

"I was undercover with the FBI. We knew diamonds were being smuggled and we had our eye on Marion and John Jacks before they moved here but we couldn't prove it. When Jacks moved to Brilliant and Marion came on as the librarian, we knew we needed eyes in the community so I moved in and took up residence as your slow-talking neighbor next door," Rock explained.

Hanna took Rock's arm. "And I joined my dad on the police force. It was the perfect setup."

"You're in the FBI too?" Jezabelle stared at Hanna. "Little Hanna is in the FBI? Did you know?" Jezabelle asked Hank.

Hank shook his head, "No, it seems they kept more than one secret from me."

Miranda's head was spinning with plots for her book. "And what does that mean?"

"It appears that my daughter and Rock Stone are married. For five years, they kept it secret. I always wondered where she disappeared to when she wasn't at her apartment, but she said she needed time away because of police work and I had no reason not to believe her," Hank explained.

Hanna stepped forward. "And my visits to Rock were twofold. We had to keep an eye on Annabelle's property. We knew they were using it for something. We saw the lights in the basement too. We were keeping a log of the times and things coinciding with the shipments of diamonds that we knew were being fenced through the businesses. We didn't have enough evidence to move in."

"That's where I came in," said Rock. "I had to get close to Jiffy, become part of his organization, and get him to trust me and let me in on the business. I finally was able to do that this past year. We were ready to move in when the floornapping started. I saw the floor pieces one night when Jiffy sent me to take his canned pickles with the diamonds inside to the storage room in Annabelle's house."

Miranda was busy taking notes. "But I don't understand. Why put the diamonds in the jars and the baked goods?"

"Marion was shipping out the diamonds in hollowed-out books. Junior would pick up pies for the library or canned goods and transport them to the library. Marion would take the diamonds out of the goods, put them in the hollowed-out books, and ship them out immediately. They used the frozen baked goods and the canned goods to store the diamonds so no one would find them until they were ready to ship them," Rock explained.

"But they got greedy. When they found the original diary of the Brilliant brothers in the hidden drawer of the bar, they knew or they thought they knew, there was gold out there. And they wanted it all. And that complicated our sting and pushed it back." Hanna nodded to Rock to continue.

"Fred Rally, although actually being semi-related to Jiffy, actually was an undercover agent too and he was an excellent baker. Jiffy hired him immediately. We had Fred living in Annabelle's house—no one knew. He would sneak in and out. Then Annabelle's family put the house up for sale and cleaned it out. That complicated our investigation even more. Fred had to be careful so no one found him there. Jiffy didn't know either and one night when Fred came home from baking at the Bistro, he surprised them cutting out the floor. Junior knocked him over the head and they threw him down in the basement."

"Did you know all this?" Jezabelle asked Hank.

Hank hesitated. "Once the floor heists started, they brought me up to speed on the investigation."

"And you didn't tell us?" Jezabelle raised her voice.

"You complicated things by forming this group and sticking your nose into the investigation."

Rock laughed. "Thankfully, you brought me in on it so I could keep an eye on you. And you found the missing link for Jiffy and Marion by finding the gold. You found it in *my* house. I missed it and Hanna and I looked all over! We knew there must be something here."

"It was your bra that I found, Hanna? I began to wonder about Rock because I didn't know about your secret trysts," Lizzy taunted.

Hanna laughed. "Yes I've lived there for years on and off and we were pretty good keeping it a secret until Jezabelle started staying up so late."

Rock continued, "You found the ball. You found the clues, and you put it all together."

"And I watched you and Lizzy go to Annabelle's house," said Hanna. "I knew someone had been there earlier because I saw the light. When you didn't come out, Rock was already with Jiffy so I texted him and you know the rest."

"But I was there," Miranda broke in. "I jogged down to the Bistro. Jiffy had asked me to turn on the ovens." She turned to Jezabelle. "Were your pies already baked that you gave to Jiffy?"

"Yup."

"You mean I was putting pies filled with diamonds in the oven?" Miranda asked. "We had an argument. He came in as I was doing it and he told me I put the wrong pies in."

"We heard you. We were downstairs. We thought it was you." Lizzy turned to Jezabelle. "One thing we were right about."

"I could have saved you. Why didn't you signal me?" Miranda chided the women.

Jezabelle rolled her eyes. "We didn't know we were in trouble yet."

"What happens now to the gold stone we found?" Phoebe's eyes gleamed, thinking of ways to spend the money.

"It's too early to tell. According to the book that Jiffy had, the Brilliant brothers' intention was for the gold to go to the city of Brilliant to benefit the town if his children didn't find it, but we have more questions we don't have answers for so it will take some time to sort it out," Hank explained.

Jezabelle stood up, a twinkle in her eye. "Does it explain where the Brilliant brothers and their families disappeared to? Why did they leave? Does it explain why only one grave had the gold? And why did they use the names of their wives? Did the wives die or were they in on the puzzle?"

Miranda put her pencil down. "And what about the other brothers? We know the brothers were named Braxton, Barton, Bennet, Bertrand, Broderick." She stopped to look at her notes. "Bartholomew and Barnabas and we know they all lived in our houses. We don't know if all were married, if all were puzzle masters, or if they had any family."

"We know the three brothers, Braxton, Barton and Bennet are the ones who concocted the cemetery puzzle, but what if the other brothers left a puzzle too?" Lizzy asked.

Rock Stone held up his hands. "Stop, it's over! The end. I have officially retired from the Penderghast Puzzle Protectors."

"Well, Mr. FBI man." Hanna kissed him on the cheek. "Do you want to tell them the rest of your news?"

"I'll be watching all of you. Hanna and I have retired from the FBI and joined the Brilliant Police Force. If there are any more puzzles to be solved from here on in, they will be by us," Rock announced.

"Were the Brilliant brothers so brilliant and hid things so well that no one who has come before us ever realized that the entire town is a mystery and a puzzle? That is the question," Jezabelle answered Rock's news with her own question.

"I am puzzled." Warbler grinned.

"For every question, there is an answer." Lizzy nodded her head.

"It's not over until it's over." Miranda drew a large explanation point on her paper.

"Well, if we don't get any of the gold, do we get some of the diamonds?" Phoebe wasn't letting go of the gold.

Rock took Phoebe's hand, walked her over to Miranda, took Miranda's pen and put it in Phoebe's hand, guided Phoebe's hand, and drew a large X over the question mark and declared, "The end."

The End

ABOUT THE AUTHOR

"I always had a dream of becoming an actress or an author. The adults in my life would call them 'pipe dreams.' Imagination always got me in trouble and people didn't take me too seriously. Add that to the fact that I had blonde hair and the title 'ditsy blonde' could be heard in teasing. As an adult, I married, raised my children and settled into careers that were respected, finally becoming a computer technician and owning my own computer business, selling and repairing computers. People took me seriously and gave me respect for my knowledge of computers. During these years, I used my creativity in my children's activities and volunteer positions, writing Christmas programs and Lenten services for our church. I hid the poems and writing I wrote as a teenager and young adult and put them out of my mind because a writing career was a dream. I believed what I had been told, that it was a 'pipe dream.'

During my life, I was an avid reader, starting out with Trixie Beldon, Nancy Drew, and expanding my world with romances, mysteries, inspirational reading and gritty crime stories. I was in awe of the talent of the authors. In 2005, I took the chance of sending my thoughts to an area newspaper and they accepted me as a columnist for their paper. I have been writing my column *Something About Nothing* since then. I write about anything that comes to mind, sometimes meaningful and sometimes fluffy and about nothing, but just silly.

In 2011, during an illness that laid me low, I began to write a story on my blog about a silly fictional town in Minnesota with an older woman character that defied our idea of old age. Each day I would wake up with a new chapter in my head. This story got me out of my illness and back into the world along with the help of good doctors and many encouraging friends. One day, I was reading a book that sounded somewhat like the book I wrote. It was a cozy mystery. I didn't know what a cozy mystery was. I looked it up, found the publisher, sent in a query letter and got accepted after a few changes to my book. Being accepted for publication by Cozy Cat Press began a new life for me. I now have four books out in the Fuchsia, Minnesota, series, two books out in the *Granny Is In Trouble* series for kids and my first book published with some of my earlier columns.

I feel truly blessed in my life. A year ago, I quit my computer business to write full time and I hope to have many more book ideas swirling around in my mind. I now know I need to have faith in myself and listen to the whispers in my heart. Creativity and imagination are a blessing and I encourage others to never give up on their dream, no matter their age."

——Julie Seedorf

Other Works by Julie Seedorf

Fuchsia, Minnesota, Series
Granny Hooks A Crook
Granny Skewers A Scoundrel
Granny Snows A Sneak
Granny Forks A Fugitive

Granny's in Trouble Series
Whatchamacallit? Thingamajig?
Snicklefritz

Anthologies and Group Mysteries
We Go On: Charity Anthology for Veterans
    published by Kiki Howel
Chasing the Codex
    published by Cozy Cat Press

Websites
    http://julieseedorf.com
    http://sprinklednotes.com
    http://thecozycatchronicles.com
    http://www.facebook.com/julie.seedorf.author
    http://www.twitter.com/julieseedorf

Made in the USA
Charleston, SC
09 May 2016